PITCH IN HIS HAIR

PITCH

Doubleday & Company, Inc., Garden City, New York, 1954

N HIS HAIR

by Faye L. Mitchell

ILLUSTRATED BY PERS CROWELL

Library of Congress Catalog Card Number 54–5901
Copyright, 1954, by Faye L. Mitchell
Printed at the Country Life Press, Garden City, N.Y.
All Rights Reserved.   First Edition

PITCH IN HIS HAIR

CHAPTER **One**

"All my work is done, Mother. May I go to the Bluff and watch for Father?" As she spoke, Abigail reached for her cape and hood that hung on a peg by the door.

Her mother looked up from the bread she was kneading. "Is the wood box filled? And is there enough dry bark so I can get coals quickly in the fireplace? I'll want to put the bread to bake in about an hour."

"Yes, Mother, and the spare room is all ready. I even put a big bunch of elderberry in my pitcher and put it on their little table. The red berries are so bright and pretty."

"Don't have your feelings hurt if they move it. They will need all the space there is. What about Jack's bed?"

"Henry put up a frame in his room in the barn, and now he is filling a straw tick. It's low enough so that Henry can roll it out of the way under his bed in the daytime. Everything looks fine; I just know the Watsons will want to stay out West. They will surely see that Washington Territory is the best place in the world! Henry says that if people stay out West long enough so that the trees drop pitch on their hair, then they want to live here always. I know a tree that has lots of pitch that gets soft and drips when the sun shines on it."

Her mother laughed. "Abby, you are a little goose. Now I suppose you are planning to get the Watson family under the tree on a warm day?"

Abby grinned. "It might work, you know."

"Don't forget that this Territory is very different from any place they have lived. You can't imagine what our old home in Vermont was like—lovely green fields, and rolling hills; not these big mountains with snow all year, and the trees that almost shut out the sky. . . ." Mother stopped her work and looked out of the window as if she could see her old home. "Even Kansas, where they've been for five years, has lots more people. Of course, we don't have Indian raids any more, but remember that Washington has been a territory less than twenty years."

Abby sighed. "I know, but if they stay you and Aunt Ellen would have good times and I'd have Jack to play with."

"Jack is fourteen, I think, and has been working like a man. He may not want to play with a girl so much younger."

"I'll play with you, Abby," Clara said, getting up from the corner where she had been playing.

Abby started to smile at her little sister, then groaned. "Mother, look! Clara has my Queen Susan box!"

"Yes, I gave it to her. I've been so busy today, Abby, all that extra baking and other cooking. I gave her those a while ago to keep her amused."

"Mother!" Abby knew better than to argue, but she

whispered fiercely to Clara as she got down on the floor by the scattered trinkets. "If you ever break these, or lose them, I'll never . . ." What could she threaten? She had to play with Clara and take care of her when Mother told her to. "I'll never tell you stories after we go to bed for a week—maybe a month."

"You make too much fuss about those beads, Abby," Mother said.

Abby didn't answer, but went on picking up the beads. She knew that if she talked when she was angry, she said too much. But these trinkets were all the jewelry she had except the coral beads and matching bracelet that Grandmother Conner had sent her for her birthday last year. Anyway, the Queen Susan things were different. The old Indian woman had given them to Abby because they were friends, because Abby had helped her.

There were blue beads from the Hudson's Bay Company trading post; the copper bracelets and earrings were from Vancouver Island, Queen Susan told her. Three bracelets were of silver; they had come from China long, long ago, with the traders who had taken furs from this very part of the United States. They were cut into queer designs and made Abby want to see the people who had made them.

She put the trinkets into the little box that Henry said came from Montreal. His father, a French *voyageur*, had given it to Henry's Indian mother when he married her at the Hudson Bay fort. Abby carefully placed the box at the back of the mantel.

11

"Better get your things on," Mother said. "I don't think it's too early to go. Father planned to get as far as Jackson's courthouse last night and start out early today. But if they don't come soon, don't wait. Remember it gets dark by five these days. Wrap Baby up, and don't forget she can't walk as fast as you."

"Don't you think it's too cold for her, Mother? It's raining—she's so slow. . . ." Mother only smiled, so Abby began to bundle Clara up. "Come along, nuisance," she said.

Clara laughed. Even if she was only four, she had learned that Abby never scolded long.

The two girls were so bundled in their homespun capes and hoods that the rain could reach just their faces and some of Clara's curls that wouldn't "stay put." Along the path the broad green leaves of the salal bushes and the gay, prickly ones of the Oregon grape brushed water on their woolen stockings and heavy shoes, but they didn't feel it.

Abby, pushing through a short cut in the woods, was stopped by a wail from Clara. "Abby, you go too fast, wait for me."

"Oh, hurry, Clara," Abby answered impatiently. "I want to get to the Bluff so we can see the wagon cross the river on the ferry. You know, when Father went to Cowlitz Landing day before yesterday he said he would get home today before dark; it's nearly time. I hope the Portland steamer wasn't late yesterday."

As Abby waited for her sister she looked back down

the trail. She could see the smoke rising from their chimney through the trees, and knew just how the house looked in its little clearing. Surely the Watsons would think it was beautiful! She guessed hardly anyone in the Territory had a better home. The heavy peeled logs made it look so solid. Now that Father had built the North Room for storing things, there were the three rooms downstairs and two tiny ones above.

All the windows were made of glass, and as for the fireplace—the neighbors said their fireplace couldn't be beat. It was large enough to take in big logs, and it never smoked even when the wind was blowing, or when you pulled the coals to the front so you would bake the bread on them.

Father had ordered a tiny iron cookstove sent from Portland in the spring. The pipe from it ran into a hole he made in the fireplace chimney. Cooking on the stove was fine in summer, for then the house didn't get so warm; but Abby was sure there was nothing so good as the fireplace for regular cooking.

The kitchen was papered in newspapers. Every year when Father pasted new ones on, he threatened to put them upside down, so Abby wouldn't go around reading them while she wiped the dishes.

Grandmother Conner had sent cloth from Vermont to cover the walls of Father's and Mother's room. Abby loved the tiny rosebuds scattered over it. Mother thought it was extravagant to put it on the walls; she said there was enough to make dresses for the three of them. But

13

Father put it on the walls; he said they could enjoy it every day, not just when they wore the dresses.

Abby knew it wasn't right to be proud, but she was glad they had such a nice house where their relatives could visit. Aunt Ellen had written that their sod house in Kansas was beginning to crumble and was hard to keep clean.

"Got your breath, now, Chubby?" Abby asked. "Then take my hand and come along. Look, there is the mill; we'll cut through here to the road. It's only a little way farther to the church, and the Bluff. Don't you want to watch for the ferry?"

Clara nodded and Abby began to advise her. "Remember, Baby, Uncle John lost his leg in the Battle of Vicksburg. He was a Union soldier, and they won, but he doesn't want to talk about it. You mustn't let on that you notice he has only one leg, that wouldn't be polite. It was a long time ago, but he still feels bad about it 'cause he can't work so hard. And we don't talk about how the grasshoppers came to Kansas and ate everything the Watsons had."

"Did the hoppers—eat—their—house?" Walking and talking made Clara puff.

"No, silly. Grasshoppers eat wheat, and garden stuff, and there isn't enough left for people, so they go hungry. Then last year the sun burned things up so Uncle John listened to Aunt Ellen and Mother and said he would move out West. We must be very nice to them, and maybe they'll like it well enough so they stay out here in

Washington Territory." Abby decided it was better to talk to her little sister about things, even if she only answered "Uh-huh," than to talk to herself.

"You see, Clara, I want them to live out here always. It isn't just to have Jack to play with; I'm getting too old to play very much. But if Aunt Ellen and Uncle John settle near here, then Mother won't be lonesome for her old home. And then Father would say that I could go away to school, because Aunt Ellen could help Mother if she needed someone. And I could learn to be a teacher. You will be as good as you can, won't you?"

"Yes," Clara said, but Abby was afraid it didn't mean much.

The mill was running, and the buzz and whine of the saw were so interesting that Abby decided they could watch a log going through. She explained to Clara that Mr. Davis had a new saw that could cut several boards from one log at one time. They watched the log riding against the saws that were fastened into one handle.

A man who was at one end smiled and waved at them, but there was so much noise they didn't know what he said. He fastened a chain around the log. "That is to keep the boards from scattering when they get cut," Abby explained. "Henry and I were here the other day and he told me about it. They call this a gang saw; I suppose because it is a bunch of saws working together. Come on, now, we can't stand here gawking all day." Abby held Clara's hand tight. The noise of the saws was almost scary, and she knew that it would be easy to get hurt in a mill.

As they came near the blacksmith shop they heard the clang of the hammer on the anvil. There was Mr. Gordon shoeing one of the Mills' horses. He kept them ready for the stagecoach, so they could have a fresh team if they wanted it. They always did if they had been climbing through the mud up Pomphrey's Mountain. Abby had often heard the men telling about it—one time a passenger from New York had been hopping mad because he had to get out and walk. She wished that Clara wasn't along, for Mr. Gordon might let her work the bellows to keep the fire hot in the forge. But if she didn't hold on to Clara there was no telling what she might do. Children were a nuisance.

"We'd better go on," she told Clara. "You walk so slow and I want to get on the Bluff." Abby hurried her up the hill and to the church. They climbed around the rosebushes, and the blackberries, and stood on the very edge looking down the valley to the river.

Abby liked to come to this place where she could see for miles on every side. There was one good thing about being with Clara, she could explain things to her little sister and feel important.

"The reason they named this place 'Claquato,' " she began, "is because in Indian language that means high ground, and you see this is a very high place. Look, see those hills 'way over there? An ocean is on the other side of them."

"What's a noshun?" Clara asked.

"An ocean," Abby corrected her. Maybe she'd better practice teaching on Clara. "An ocean is a large body of water. That means there is lots and lots of water, not just like this river. I'm going to ride on it in a big ship some-day."

"I'll go with you," Clara said.

Abby sighed. "We'll see, when the time comes. You can't go everywhere with me, Clara. Someday I'll go away to school and then to teach . . ."

Clara began to cry. "I don't want you to go away and leave me, Abby."

"Oh, for goodness sake!" Abby couldn't help giving her a little shake. "You act as if I had gone away already. Look over there—down in that valley is the Judson farm and the road to Boisfort. Now on this side—oh see! There, that must be Father's wagon, just getting on the ferry. Let's watch them come across. You can't see it but there is a wheel fastened to a tall tree on this side. A rope goes through it and to the ferry—oh, someday you can go and watch the man wind the rope, maybe. Now they are almost across. Let's run down the Military Road and meet them. Mother won't care; it's very early."

They hurried down the steep hill, stumbling in and out of the deep ruts. Abby carried Clara over the worst places. The rain had almost stopped, but the road was slippery and some places the mud was sticky. That means a lot of shoe cleaning tomorrow, Abby thought.

As they stood waiting at the foot of the hill, she began

to feel shy. After all, these people were strangers, even if they were relatives, and it might be hard to talk to them.

Aunt Ellen must be nice, for she was Mother's sister. She had written that Uncle John was moody. Abby wasn't sure just what that meant, but it sounded queer. Jack might turn out to be a tease, like some of those boys at school. If she fought with him, then likely the Watsons would go back to Kansas. She sighed, then laughed. As Henry always told her, no use scratching the fleas before they got on you! But Jack had just better not make fun of her pets—the little fawn and the bear cub and the baby wildcat. If he teased them he could go back to Kansas and good riddance to bad rubbish.

When the wagon came near, Father called, "Whoa! Whoa, there!" as if Tim and Sally were trying to run away. Aunt Ellen leaned down from the seat and said "Hello" so happily that Abby forgot she was a stranger.

"Here's the welcoming committee!" Father teased. "Abby seems to think she just about discovered the old Oregon Country, so of course she has to get out and greet people. This is Clara," he said as Abby boosted her sister over the wheel so she could climb to the seat where Uncle John and Aunt Ellen sat with Father. "You can see she's about as broad as she is long. She's a pretty good girl, except when her curls are being combed. And this is Abby. I haven't any boy, but Abby takes the place of one; she can just about run the farm. Tries sometimes to run me, too."

Abby grinned happily as she climbed up and stood behind the seat. Jack was standing there, but he didn't smile, just grunted and moved over a little when she said "Hello." Abby hoped he had heard Father bragging about her, then he'd know she wasn't just a child. She was afraid to look straight at him, but the glimpse she had had certainly wasn't very pleasant.

Aunt Ellen cuddled Clara on her lap. "This poor baby! She is all wet, and I'm afraid she's cold. Abby, too. They oughtn't to come out in the rain, although it's nice to get such a welcome!" She kissed Clara and smiled back at Abby.

"Rain!" Father laughed. "These children don't mind rain. Why, we grow webs between our toes, just like ducks."

"Lots of times it doesn't rain," Abby broke in. She knew Father might start telling some of his rain stories and they might believe them and get scared away before they were settled.

Uncle John turned and smiled at her. "I'm sure it doesn't," he said. He hadn't spoken before, but when he smiled, Abby thought it was just like the sun coming out.

Standing behind them, she could look at them and not seem to stare. It was funny that her uncle's hair was so white, for he was just about Father's age. Must have been the war, she decided. His face was thin and sad until he smiled.

Mother and Aunt Ellen looked very much alike. They both had light brown hair that had probably been yellow like Clara's when they were little. And it was curly, too. Abby loved her father, but she would have liked to have curls like Mother's and Clara's instead of straight, almost red hair like Father's.

Jack didn't look like either of them, she saw. By pretending to point out the church as they climbed the hill, she could look at him. His hair was straight and black, and his eyes were black, too. She hoped the boys at school wouldn't call him Indian Jack!

As they jolted over the ruts, Abby held tight to the back of the seat. Aunt Ellen's jacket brushed against her hands; it was so smooth, and the blue was almost like a bluejay's back. There was a collar of soft black fur, and she wore a toque of the same fur. Abby wished Mother had something pretty like that. She still wore the same coat she had worn when they came out West in the sixties.

"Did you have a good trip, Aunt Ellen?" she asked. Mother had explained that you should always ask people that when they came from a journey.

"Well, Abigail, it was all interesting, and some of it was very nice. We enjoyed the ride on the railway from Denver to San Francisco; that was a new experience for Jack and me. I'll admit I was a little frightened when they went fast—one man said they were going twenty-five miles an hour on straight stretches."

"My!" Abby said. "That would scare me. Just think, Father, we could get to Olympia in about an hour from our place! Please, Aunt Ellen, when you have time, tell me about trains. We are going to have a railroad through here someday, up from Cowlitz Landing. And Governor Stevens, he was our first governor, planned a route all the way back East."

"I wish they had a train so we could go back to Kansas on it next spring," Jack said suddenly.

"Well, you can talk! I thought you didn't know how." Abby flared at him. "But—maybe you won't go back!" She was cross because her voice shook.

"Abby!" her father said quietly, and she felt her face get red.

"Oh, we'll go back!" Jack's chin went up and his black eyes snapped as he answered positively. "I know we won't like it out here. I like to ride my horse fast over the prairies; not poke around stumps and through trees the way these roads are. And we don't have rain all the time, the way it is here, and——"

"Never mind, Jack." Uncle John didn't talk loud, but Jack stopped. He scowled at Abby and she stuck her tongue out at him.

"Look," Father said, "that's our grove of trees ahead. One more bend in the road—there, now, you can see the house."

"It's beautiful!" Aunt Ellen told them, and Abby knew she would love her.

"Solid-looking," Uncle John said. "That fireplace looks like Vermont."

"A Vermonter made it," Father reminded him. "Hulloo! Julia! Here are some tired and hungry people!"

Mother came running before he had finished calling. Aunt Ellen climbed out of the wagon and the two women hugged and kissed each other and even cried a little while they were laughing. Abby wiped her eyes; she realized now how lonely Mother had been. She hadn't seen any of her family since she and Father left Vermont the year before the War between the States. If the Watsons would only decide to live here!

Finally Father said, "Listen, we have a house, you don't have to stand out here in the rain gabbing. And don't try to say everything in ten minutes; everybody will be here tomorrow. You all go in, and Jack and I will unload what you need tonight."

As she followed the others into the house, Abby noticed that Jack shivered and looked unhappy. My goodness, she thought, I'll have to watch my tongue for a few days. I wish I knew how I could make him like this place.

Two

Aunt Ellen was really going to be nice to have around, Abby decided. When they went into the house, her aunt said, "What a beautiful room! I've missed having a fireplace all the time we were in Kansas, but can you really afford to have so much wood on at once?"

The others laughed, but Jack muttered, "Wood! That's all there is out here. How do you get it dry enough to burn?"

Abby pretended she didn't hear him. She pulled a chair to the corner of the hearth and made Uncle John sit down. Aunt Ellen was sniffing at the steam from the kettles on the fire and saying that she was really hungry.

Father and Jack brought in the satchels and bundles from the wagon and put them under the stairs.

"We'll leave the trunks in the wagon until morning," Father said. "Come on, Jack, you and I will drive down to the barn and unhitch and see whether there are any chores still to be done."

Jack didn't answer. He followed Father slowly, and looked longingly at the fire as he went out. Abby shook her head. She liked people not to talk too much, for that gave her more chance, but Jack carried this shut-mouth business too far. She hoped he would be better when he felt more at home.

Mother took Aunt Ellen up to the room the Watsons were to have, and Clara tagged after them.

As she started up, Mother called, "Now, Abigail, pull some coals over the Dutch oven, the bread is almost baked. And watch the other things that are cooking while you get the table set. Bring the things from the North Room."

When Mother said "Abigail" instead of "Abby" it meant that she had to be very careful for she had responsibility. Probably she'd better not even try to entertain Uncle John, but just hurry to get him something to eat.

She swung the big iron kettle that hung from a rod across the fireplace over near the center, so the meat would finish cooking. Venison, she thought, as the fragrant steam puffed out from around the cover. With a shovel she lifted bright bark coals and put them on the lid of the Dutch oven, then pulled more coals around it. She peeked in a third kettle and saw squash. When she tried it with a big fork, she found it was tender, so she pulled it to the edge of the hearth so it would keep warm but not burn. Potatoes were baking in the ashes at the front. She stuck a fork into them, and when steam came out she knew they were done.

As she stood up, she saw that Uncle John was watching her.

He smiled. "You seem to know how to cook."

"I like to cook in the fireplace. I think things taste better, don't you? Of course, it's nice to have that little stove in the summer, and sometimes we have so much that Mother uses it in the winter, but I like this better."

She lighted a candle and went into the North Room to get butter and cream; she saw that Mother had made huckleberry pie and camas cakes. Well, they were going to start the Watsons off with a good meal; if Jack was like most boys he'd feel better when he got some food sticking to his ribs. She took a big pitcher of milk to the table, then hurried to put the coffee on; she had almost forgotten that.

In the North Room again for jam, Abby held the candle up and looked around. That was something she did every evening; the North Room made her feel so safe. It was snug. Father had built it of logs, like the rest of the house. Then he brought boards from the Davis mill and made a lining for the room a few inches from the wall. He filled this space with sawdust, and the room was cool in summer, and never freezing in winter.

When he had it all finished, Father said to Mother, "Well, there's your room. It cost as much as a cow."

Mother said it would save what the cow gave—milk and butter and cheese, as well as lots of other things.

Abby let the candlelight fall on the things around the room—wooden kegs of butter, eggs buried in meal, pork in brine, ham and bacon hanging from the ceiling, bins around the wall filled with apples and vegetables. It seemed silly to worry about whether crops would be good, or, if they were, whether the deer would jump the fence and eat things. As long as the North Room looked this way, she wasn't going to be doleful. She put down the candle, picked up the jam, and tiptoed out. It was peaceful, like being in a church.

Uncle John was sitting, staring sadly into the fire, so Abby put the dishes down quietly, and then went to stand by him. "When you get rested, come and look in the North Room. It's chock full of food, and always makes me feel that things are going to turn out all right."

He smiled and patted the hand she had laid on his shoulder. "That's one of the nice things about being young, Abby. You feel that you can make things turn out right."

"Oh, no, Uncle John! It isn't because I'm young. Everybody in Washington Territory knows that you can make things work right out here!"

Her uncle laughed, and Abby thought, There, I wanted him to laugh—and he did. It shows you can make things go right.

When Father and Jack came in, Mother and Aunt Ellen were still upstairs, laughing and jabbering. Father pretended to be cross. "You girls still foolin' around?" he called out loudly. Then he shook his head at Uncle. "Well, John, looks like Ellen and Julia will talk all the time and never get us anything to eat. Lucky Abby is a good cook."

Mother came down the ladder stairs in a rush and laughed at him. "Don't grumble; you've never starved yet. Supper's all ready. Where's Henry?"

"He's finishing the chores; he'll be here right away."

Aunt Ellen was coming down the stairs backwards. "These are like the ones on the ship, so steep and narrow. But at least they stand still while I go up and down and don't swing around like those on the ship. My, they were hard to manage! Who is Henry? Did you write about him?"

"Henry?" Mother answered as she lifted the venison on a wooden platter and gave Abby the thickening to stir into the gravy. "He's an old man who came to live with us last year. That is, he lives here when he doesn't get restless and go off hunting or fishing. His name is Henry Peltier. His father was a French Canadian who worked for the Hudson's Bay Company; his mother was an Indian."

"You'll like him," Abby told Jack, who was watching her stirring the gravy with a long wooden spoon. "He was born at Fort Nisqually, on the Sound, but he's been all over the Territory, and even to China. He can do anything, prospect for gold, hunt, fish . . ."

Father chuckled. "Good thing I'm not a jealous man, John. My wife likes having Henry around to tell stories since we don't have many books and magazines. And Abby sits for hours listening to his yarns. I'm going to forget how to talk."

"If you haven't forgotten how to eat, come to the table," Mother said.

"Come and get it!" Father called. "That's the way they call the men to eat in the logging camps," he explained to Jack.

Mother and Father sat on chairs at the ends of the table; tonight Mother pulled another chair up so Aunt Ellen could sit by her. Jack had a place between Abby and Clara on a bench at one side. Henry came in just as they were getting settled, and after Father introduced him sat down on the other bench with Uncle John.

Abby looked happily around. Everyone except Jack was smiling, and even he looked pleasant. The lamp that Father had given Mother for Christmas a year before sat in the center of the table and gave a soft light. The candles on the mantel burned brighter than usual, she was certain. Once when she got up to pour more coffee, she threw a small fir branch into the fireplace. The flames lighted the whole room, and the pleasant piney smell was just right.

"Don't slide on the bench," she whispered to Jack. "This is a new one; Father hasn't had time to smooth it yet; you'll get splinters."

"Guess these breeches can stand it." He answered gruffly, but he looked more friendly, and almost smiled.

"What a supper!" Aunt Ellen said. "I never ate bread cooked in a fireplace before; it's wonderful. Where do you get this flour?"

"Waterbury, down at the Davis mill, grinds as good flour as you'll find anywhere," Mother answered.

"What's this meat?" Jack asked Abby. His mouth was full, and he had taken three helpings. Certainly he was enjoying the food in Washington Territory, she thought.

"Venison—deer meat. Didn't you ever eat any?"

He shook his head. "Ate some buffalo meat once, but it was tough. Do you eat bears out here? Read they were tough."

"Sometimes we eat bear," Father told him. "But it's the way you cook meat that makes it tender. Your aunt Julia can do anything with that iron kettle over coals in the fireplace. Once, I remember, she got hold of some leather I was aiming to use to make Abby some shoes. She got it so tender that we ate it and I had to hunt up some more for the shoes."

Aunt Ellen laughed. "Seems good to hear you yarning again, Will. Like old times."

Father sighed. "Ellen, you misjudge me. 'Yarning,' the very idea. Wait until you hear Henry. He tells yarns. My stories are true. But talking about meat, Jack, bears are all right if they aren't too old. Now there's a cub that I spotted that ought to be good eating come, say, Thanksgiving."

"Father! No!" Abby wailed.

"Don't tease her, William." Mother shook her head at him.

"What does your father mean?" Jack asked in a low voice while the others were talking.

"Henry brought a darling little bear cub in from the woods. He helped me make a pen for him, but Mother says I'll have to take him out and turn him loose; he is getting rough. I'll take him 'way back into the woods; maybe he won't get shot."

Jack gave her an admiring look. "Say, Abby, you're

31

almost as good as a boy! Do you have any other animals in your pen?"

"Yes, there's a fawn. And I have a baby wildcat that Mother doesn't want me to keep either. You see, Henry hunts a good deal. He doesn't intend to shoot the mothers that have little babies, but sometimes he does; then he brings the babies home for me to take care of. I'll show them to you tomorrow. And I'm not almost as good as a boy, I'm better." She got up and went to the North Room for pies before he could answer.

Soon Jack was too busy eating huckleberry pie to ask

questions but his mother wanted to know what the berries were and where they came from.

"These are fresh huckleberries," Mother said. "Abby picks them in the woods and in some of the clearings. We have some put up for next winter. We put them in bottles that I fill with water. Then I boil them and put in corks Abby whittles from corncobs. Seal them with paper dipped in white of egg and they keep fine."

"I watch for bottles along the Military Road," Abby said. "Whiskey bottles. Men that go from Cowlitz Landing to Olympia in the stagecoach often throw out the

empty bottles——" Uncle John's loud laugh stopped her. He really can laugh, she thought. Even Aunt Ellen and Father joined in, and Mother smiled. "Wha-at did I say, Uncle John?"

"Nothing, child. I'm sorry I laughed. But I thought of your grandmother Conner, back in Vermont. She's strong on temperance, always talking about it. If she knew that her namesake went along after the stagecoach picking up empty whiskey bottles—well, I can just see her, and hear her, too!" Uncle John smiled at her.

Abby thought a minute. "I don't believe Grandmother would mind. She's written me letters, and she often talks about not wasting things. And glass itself isn't bad; it's just the use they put it to. Glass in windows is a great help."

Uncle John looked at Father. "Will, if Abby were a boy I'd say that you have a lawyer on your hands; takes after her grandfather Clark, I guess. Even old Dan'l Webster couldn't have thought up a better rebuttal."

"Don't spoil her, John," Mother said.

"Well, Grandmother Conner doesn't need to worry that I'm going to drink any whiskey after what I saw it do to the geese. I'm not a goose, but whiskey might make me act that way. I don't want people making fun of me," Abby told her uncle.

"What did geese have to do with whiskey?" Jack asked.

Henry grinned. "Young feller, you took the bait in that trap. Abby wanted you to ask so she could tell the story."

"Well, the stage driver told me how it started, so I know," Abby said. "You see, a man on the coach started to take a drink and it made a woman mad. So she grabbed the bottle and threw it out of the window. That was Saturday. Sunday morning, when we came out of church, there was a string of geese waddling all over the road. Nobody knew what had happened until they found that the bottle had landed on a sack of wheat by the road. It was broken and the wheat soaked with whiskey was spilling out. It was awful funny to watch them, but I don't want to look that way."

"Speaking of Sunday," Mother said, "that is tomorrow. I know you people are tired, but if you get to bed now you'll feel like going to church tomorrow."

"Let me help with the work. . . ." Aunt Ellen began to gather up the dishes.

"No," Mother said, "Abby and I can hustle through these. Will, you carry up the rest of their things."

"If you are short of room, I could sleep by this fire," Uncle John said.

Aunt Ellen patted his shoulder. "Wait until you see our room upstairs!"

"We made a new mattress for your bed this summer," Abby told him. "It's stuffed with moss I gathered in the woods. And there is a feather bed made with wild duck feathers."

"I'll be up there in two shakes," her uncle said. "Good night!"

Abby watched, and thought it was wonderful the way

he could go so fast with his peg leg. He was whistling "Arkansas Traveler" as he climbed. She heard Aunt Ellen whisper to Mother.

"Julia, John hasn't acted so happy in years as he has tonight. What have you done to him?"

Abby wanted to say that people were happy in Washington Territory, but Jack interrupted.

"Where do I sleep, Aunt Julia?"

"Poor Jack!" his aunt said. "Did you think you were forgotten? Henry has a bed made up for you in his room in the barn attic."

Henry took Jack by the arm. "Come on, young feller, we have the best place of all; no stuffy house for us. Someday I'll take you on a hunting trip. We'll take a tarp and sleep on fir branches under some tree."

Jack was smiling as the two left the room. Abby scowled. Henry had never offered to take her on a hunting trip. Just because Jack was a boy he had the best of things. She was sure she knew better how to act in the woods than he did. She clattered the dishes into the pan and began to wash. Mother helped clear away the food and set the table for breakfast. She took the lamp into their bedroom, where Father was putting Clara to bed.

Abby spread a cloth over the table and went out into the yard to throw out her dishwater.

The rain was over. She peered up between the tall fir trees. Sure enough, there was a star she could wish on.

"I hope they stay," she whispered. "Uncle John is very nice; Aunt Ellen is nice, and I think Jack may improve."

She heard her mother call, "Come, Abby."

"Yes, Mother," she answered, but she stood, swinging her empty pan and thinking. Of course, she wasn't really superstitious; she knew that putting pitch wouldn't really work, but still . . . Henry believed some of those things, and he was awful smart. She didn't need to say anything about it, but she decided to get a little pitch, have it warm, and put a tiny bit down at the end of Aunt Ellen's long hair. Or maybe it would be better to put it in Jack's; he'd think he got it himself from the woods. It was plain as the eyes on an owl that whatever Jack wanted, his mother wanted him to have. So Jack was the first one she'd trap.

"Abigail!"

"Coming, Mother." Before her mother could mention her dawdling in the yard, Abby began to talk.

"Mother, why is it that Jack doesn't look like either his father or mother? Clara looks like you, and I look like father, but Jack doesn't look like anybody I know."

Her mother hesitated. "Well, I haven't told you this, for I thought maybe the Watsons didn't talk about it— and I knew you would if you knew it. But Aunt Ellen said this evening that Jack knows it, so I suppose . . ."

"Knows what?" Abby never could see why her mother went all around Robin Hood's barn to get to a point.

"You see, when your uncle John was going home after he was injured in the war—he'd been in the hospital, you know—well, he had to ride during the night and hide during the day. And one day he stopped in a ruined house on the Blue Ridge Mountains and he heard a child crying. He hunted and there was Jack. He was about four years old, scared to death, and starved."

"The poor little boy!" Abby understood why Jack looked so sad.

"So, Uncle John took care of him and took him back to Vermont, riding on his mule! Ellen tells me that they found last year that Jack's father and mother were killed by raiders, so now they have adopted him and they think of him as their own boy."

CHAPTER **Three**

Abby went quietly up to bed, not even taking a candle, so she wouldn't disturb her aunt and uncle. The partitions between the rooms were thin, and she could hear them snoring, so she hoped they were resting. Clara was curled in the middle of their bed, as usual. Abby cuddled her sister and thought about what her mother had told her. Maybe that was why Jack was so stiff—he was shy and didn't feel that he belonged in the family. Abby decided to be very good to him and plan things that would make him happy. She wouldn't even fuss about Henry's taking him hunting.

She yawned as she planned, and then heard her mother call.

"Abigail! Hurry, dear! Breakfast is ready and the others are downstairs waiting. I want to get the work done up early. You answered me when I called you a while ago."

Abby rubbed her eyes. It was morning—when had she gone to sleep? She jumped out of bed as she answered.

"I'll be down in a minute. I must have answered in my sleep. I'll dress Clara." She lighted a candle and woke Clara. They talked as Abby combed and braided her long hair and ran the comb through Clara's curls.

"Don't cry," she scolded. "Here, put your moccasins on and go down to breakfast. You can get dressed later."

Then she slipped into her gingham work dress, giggling as she remembered part of the dream she was having when Mother called.

It seemed she had taken Jack out to see her pets and he had tried to ride the fawn. The baby cougar jumped to his shoulder and dug his claws in so Jack howled. It was funny now, but in the dream she had been scared.

She washed quickly and helped put the ham and eggs on the table. Mother had fried the potatoes on the little stove, and made the coffee there, too.

Mother apologized because she had slept late and there was no hot bread. Father laughed. They would have to go hungry, he guessed, but it was a good thing there was some pie left from last night, and here were cookies. He knew a Vermonter liked something of that sort.

"Fill up the cracks with these," he said to Jack.

While they ate, Mother told the Watsons about the Claquato community. "We have almost the first church built in Washington Territory. Mr. and Mrs. Davis gave the land and the lumber, and the settlers at Boisfort furnished the interior. I guess that everyone helped to buy the bell; it was made in Boston and cost a hundred dollars. Everybody wanted to help; the Territory was only five years old then, in 1858, but the people wanted a church."

"I had a glimpse of it as we drove along yesterday,"

Uncle John said. "Doesn't it have an unusual steeple?"

Mother laughed. "Yes, Mr. Clinger carved a wooden crown of thorns like one he had seen in Portland. We use the church for a school, too."

"Jack, if you help Henry with the feeding, I'll milk and we can get through quickly."

"Hurry with the work and then we can see the pets," Abby whispered to her cousin. "I'll go out as soon as I finish here."

She and Aunt Ellen whisked through the dishes, and then Abby went out to the yard. Jack was at the pen playing with the bear cub. Abby had to cuff the baby cougar; he was always jealous when she petted the bear cub too long. She gave them their feed, and then went to another pen where she had chickens. The turkeys flew down from the trees, where they had been roosting. Two geese and three ducks waddled up in a solemn line from the pond below the barn.

After she had fed the poultry, Abby went to the other pen. Jack was petting the fawn and feeding it apples. Abby was holding the cougar when she heard a little quack at her feet. It was her pet duck. He was lame, but he could waddle and limp at the same time. Jack laughed, but Abby groaned.

"Oh, dear, Tilly, you're out again! I must get him shut up tight, if I don't get anything else done. Last Sunday——"

"Why do you call him Tilly if it's a he?" Jack wanted to know.

"Because his name is 'Tilicum,' that's Indian for good friend. I call him Tilly for short. You see, he was hurt when he was little, and I took care of him. Now he wants to follow me everywhere, just like a dog. He's worse than King, for he won't mind me. Last Sunday he followed me to church. I didn't think it would matter, but we had a preacher that gave an extra-long sermon. Tilly came up on the porch to look for me, and just at the end, when the preacher was very solemn and everyone was quiet, Tilly quacked and quacked. Everybody laughed. The preacher was cross and Mother scolded. Father said if it happened again we'd have roast duck in a hurry. I must shut him up tight."

Abby took Tilly to a small pen of cedar boughs she had twisted together. "I made this special pen for him so I could feed him where the others wouldn't fight him. Now it isn't strong enough to hold when he pushes."

"Do you know many Indian words?" Jack asked.

Abby smiled; he sounded almost respectful. "Oh I can talk a little Chinook jargon. Someone made that up a long time ago so the early traders could talk with the

Indians. The Chinooks were the biggest tribe, so there are more of their words, but there's some made up from French, and English. The Hudson's Bay Company had lots of French working for them."

"Did you learn it in school?"

"No, Henry taught me most of what I know and I learned some from a little Indian girl. She was picking berries in the woods where I went, and we had fun teaching each other words. She was nice; I hoped she would come back and play sometime. There aren't many Indians around here; most of them are on reservations."

"Say some jargon for me."

"One sentence you would like is *Mika tickey mucka muck.*"

"What does that mean?"

"I want something to eat!"

Jack laughed good-naturedly. "That's a good one; I'll have to remember it to say to the boys back in Kansas. I want to learn others, too."

Abby started to say that maybe he wouldn't be going back to Kansas. Then she remembered that Mother had told her not to argue with him. Anyway, she had no time, for they heard the "gong" ring. Mother kept a horseshoe hanging by the door and struck it three times when she wanted Abby, and five times for Father. She was in the door when Abby and Jack ran to the house.

"Abigail, you can finish dressing Clara, and get yourself washed and dressed. Ellen and I are starting now for church. I am going a little early; I want to see some of the

43

women and arrange for them to come for a quilting so they can meet Aunt Ellen. Your father and John have gone on so they wouldn't have to walk fast. Don't dawdle now."

Abby soon was washed and dressed; she and Clara were ready when Jack came in from the barn wearing a new suit that his mother had made from one of Uncle John's uniforms. The girls admired it, but while they were talking they heard the first bell ringing for church.

"My goodness, we'll have to hurry," Abby said. "That means we have only half an hour, and we have a mile to walk. I wish we could go horseback, but Mother won't let me take Clara that way. And she's so slow! Come on, Chubby."

They took the trail through the woods, since it was shorter and easier walking than in the deep ruts in the road.

"Let's keep a watch for bears or cougars," Jack said.

"We don't have time and they wouldn't come here anyway. You'll see plenty of bears this winter. They don't hurt anyone unless someone starts a fight or tries to bother the cubs. I don't want to see any cougars. My baby one is all right, but even it is getting a little rough. But the big ones climb a tree, go out on a limb, and then drop down on you and claw you."

"I don't want a cougar to claw me," Clara wailed.

Abby shook her impatiently. "Now, Clara, don't cry. There aren't any wildcats here. You can't cry and hurry at the same time and I don't want to be late."

"I'll take her on my shoulder," Jack said.

Clara was delighted with this plan, and they made such good time that Abby said they could rest a minute at the end of the trail before they got into Pearson's yard. She pointed out the different places in Claquato. Here in Pearson's carpenter shop they sometimes had dances after they swept up the shavings and chucked the lumber against the wall.

"Down there is the mill; it's fun to watch them saw. And there is the blacksmith's shop. Mr. Gordon lets me pump the bellows for him. That is the courthouse. . . . Listen, what is that noise?" She groaned. "Jack! What will we do?"

"What is it? What's the matter?" Then he heard the quack, quack and began to laugh.

"That Tilly!" Abby wanted to cry. Mother thought it was very wrong to be late to church. If the duck made a noise, Father would carry out his threat. And they had only a few minutes; they couldn't take time to carry Tilly home. It was just hopeless—and things had been going so well. Clara looked at her sister and started to cry.

That made Abby cross. "Keep still, Clara, you don't know what the trouble is. Jack, think fast, what can we do?"

"I don't know—yes, I do; give me your hair ribbon."

"Oh, Jack, I can't, it's the only one I have and Mother would be cross if it gets spoiled."

"Then your old duck will have to get killed—unless you have a string."

"I haven't—yes, I have. Turn around a minute." Abby took the strings that had been holding up her stockings; she'd have to trust to her long underwear to hold them up. "Here, take them; but it won't do any good to picket Tilly, he'll just quack louder."

"I'm not going to picket him." Jack made a loop in the string, put it around the duck's bill, then under its wing, and tied it about Tilly's leg.

"You are really smart," Abby said.

"He'll be uncomfortable, but he won't be hurt. He won't wander very far, either. Look, you two start on and I'll run back down the trail with Tilly, just a little way. Then he'll have farther to hobble. I'll come out as soon as church is over. Go on, I'll catch you."

Abby took Clara's hand and they went on quickly. "Don't you say a word of this to Mother, Clara, or I won't tell you any stories in bed tonight. Or tomorrow night, either."

Clara promised. Jack caught up with them as they crossed the road and the three marched into church, a little out of breath, just as the last bell was ringing.

Abby couldn't keep her mind on the sermon because she was worrying for fear Tilly would pull off the string. On every hymn she sang as loud as she could, to drown out any other noise. When Elder Griffin called for one hymn and said that they would sing all eight stanzas, Abby gave a little moan; how long would church last?

46

Then she saw Jack grinning at her and she grinned back. She was glad he was turning out better than she had thought he would last night.

Luckily, there wasn't a long sermon, and Elder Griffin always shouted so that nobody would have heard a noise from outside.

As soon as the benediction had been pronounced, Abby grabbed Clara's hand. "I'll hurry on and see about dinner, Mother. Then you and Aunt Ellen can visit with the women."

She was ashamed when Mrs. Davis patted her on the head and told Mother, "What a good little girl you have, Mrs. Conner. She seems right capable, too. Girls can't do as much work as when I was young, mostly."

Mother smiled. "Yes, Abigail is most dependable."

Abby's face was burning as she hurried Clara to the door. It wasn't fun to get credit for being good when you were really only trying to cover up a mistake. Still, the duck's getting out hadn't been all her fault.

The two girls took a short cut through Pearson's yard and started on the trail. Jack had said that he didn't want to wait around and talk to people he didn't know; that he would meet them down the trail. They found him looking for Tilly, but they couldn't see the duck and of course he couldn't quack to let them know where he was.

Finally Clara discovered Tilly sitting mournfully where he had hobbled off the path. They laughed when Tilly struck Jack with his bill when he was being untied. Then he shook his feathers and went down the path toward home as fast as he could.

"He doesn't like me, and he won't like me any better tomorrow when I fix a pen for him," Jack laughed. "Suppose we hurry now, too. Breakfast was a long time ago. What do we have for dinner?"

Abby pretended she was thinking hard. "*Icktas*," she said.

"Is that some kind of meat?"

"You wait and see; you'll like it." Then she decided not to tease. After all, Jack had saved Tilly from being roasted. "*Icktas* just means 'things'—you know, some of this and some of that. I don't know what we are going to have. Very often Henry gets dinner when we are at church. Maybe he and Mother planned it."

"Let me ride, Jack," Clara begged.

Jack swung her up to his shoulder. "Can Henry cook?" he wanted to know.

"Oh, yes, he can make a fine meal. But I promised to get home and set the table. Henry won't do that; he says it is squaw's work."

"Well, *Mika tickey mucka muck!*" Jack said, and went trotting down the trail. Clara held to his long black hair and tried to get him to go faster.

Tilly was waiting in dignified silence by his pen. Abby petted him. "Poor Tilly! He only wanted to come along with us."

"You spoil him," Jack said. "Maybe he's learned a lesson, but I'll make a pen tomorrow that he'll never get

48

out of. Now I'll stuff grass into this hole where he crawled out."

In the house they found Henry working at the fireplace. "Dinner is a surprise, Abby," he told her. "You get the table set so everything will be ready when the others get here. I told your mother that I'd rustle some grub, but I didn't say what it would be."

"What is it?" Abby went to the fireplace while she buttoned on a big coverall apron. She peeked into a kettle. "That's the dried corn that Mother started cooking last night. I see the potatoes baking . . . Oh!" She looked at the coals in the front of the fireplace. "I know! Where did you get it?"

Jack looked where she was pointing. "I don't see anything!"

He looked so disappointed that Abby told him. "It's a salmon!"

Henry pushed some of the coals away, and showed him a long roll of what looked like mud.

"I was going fishing this week," Henry told Abby. "Then when we got word the Watsons were coming, I gave it up. I didn't want to leave you and your mother here alone all night. But I told one of the Indian boys to bring me a good salmon. I got it last night—so here it is."

"I still don't see anything but mud," Jack said.

"That's right, young feller," Henry laughed. "That's all there is to see just now. We'll catch the salmon a little later."

"In that mud?" Jack shook his head. "And I'm awful hungry."

"Just you wait; you'll see," Abby advised as she hurried in and out of the North Room with bread and butter, jam, cream, and pickles. "I hear the others coming; don't you tell them; we'll let them sit down at the table first."

Uncle John came to the fireplace to warm his hands. Abby saw him looking at the stove, and the table, and then back at the fire, where only one kettle hung with steam puffing out under the lid.

She laughed. "Guess it's a good thing we had a big supper last night, Uncle John. Oh well, there's lots of bread and jam. And here are potatoes." She put them on a wooden platter and set it on the table. "Everything is ready; I'll dish up the corn. Sit down."

Everyone sat down except Henry and Abby. She brought a long wooden platter and put it down on the hearth.

Uncle John stood up again so he could see. "There's something going on here," he said.

Everyone watched while Henry pulled what looked like a roll of hard mud out on the hearth. He took a sharp knife and split it open. There lay a big salmon, pink and savory, with the skin which had protected it still in the clay.

"Looks like a big shell lined with the skin," Uncle John said. "How did you do it, Henry?"

"I got the fish all cleaned and ready last night," Henry answered. "When I came to breakfast I put a big strip of

bark on the fire so it would burn down to coals when I wanted it. I wrapped the salmon in wet cornhusks—seaweed is better but I didn't have any—then wrapped the whole thing in a special kind of clay that I found over near Mill Creek. As soon as you people left for church I put it to bake in the fireplace. And here it is!"

"And here I am," said Uncle John. "Serve the ladies fast, Will, or I'll reach over and get a chunk for myself. I haven't smelled anything so good since that venison last night."

"Here, John," Mother said, "while you're waiting, fix a baked potato with lots of butter in it. And we like this dried corn; I cook it for hours, slow, over the fire."

"Good potatoes, William," Uncle John said. "How you raise them on stump land, I don't know. There didn't seem to be five yards straight on the level in that we looked at this morning. Stumps scattered thick as flies on spilled molasses."

"It's easy to do with a grasshopper plow," Father answered. "When we get to the stumps it just hops over them and plows on the other side."

Aunt Ellen laughed. "John, you might have known that Will would have some explanation, true or not."

Abby watched Jack; he was eating, not talking. Even if he had wanted to say something, his mouth was too full. Surely he was going to think this was a good country, since the food was so good. But maybe he liked Kansas food as well. She decided there was no use worrying; better to think up some fun they could have. Last night

52

Jack had acted so glum she hadn't cared much about having him around; but this morning he was fun. Of course, Aunt Ellen was the most important one if Abby was ever to go away to school.

Henry was asking the Watsons about the train trip. That was one way that he had never traveled, and he wanted to know about it.

"You folks had it easier than we did a dozen years ago, Ellen," Father said. He always liked to tell about driving over the Oregon Trail. "In 1860 there wasn't any railroad. Remember how hot it was, Julia? A little of this rain would have been mighty pleasant."

"Still, we weren't firsts," Abby complained.

" 'Firsts'?" Uncle John asked.

"Yes. You see, settlers came here fifteen years before Father and Mother, and they always talk about who did things first. I'm not the first white child born in Lewis County, and we didn't have the first glass windows, and Father didn't set out the first fruit trees——"

"But Abby can talk more and faster than any 'first,' " Father said. "You'd think she invented Washington Territory to hear her talk."

"Your mother sent us an article from Leslie's *Illustrated News* a few years ago, Will," Aunt Ellen said. "I don't know whether she thought it would encourage us to come West or not. The writer said that the Northwest had the tallest trees, the biggest rivers, the highest mountains, and the best volcanoes on the Pacific slope."

"Volcanoes!" Abby said indignantly. "We don't have

any. Of course, Rainier used to be a volcano, and the top is still hot, I guess. Anyway, there's a little cloud cap on it when there is a rain coming."

"That cap must be about worn out," Jack said.

Abby made up her mind to cut him an extra-small piece of pie.

Uncle John suddenly handed his plate to Father. "Some more of that salmon, if you please, Will. I don't know how you feel, Jack. If you want to waste your time on Kansas catfish, you can. I'm going to stay out here and eat salmon and venison, if your mother will agree."

Abby looked anxiously at Aunt Ellen, who sat silent for a minute, then spoke slowly. "We came only yesterday, John, we don't know whether we'll like it or not. We said we'd stay a few months, long enough to see how we feel. Come spring, if you and Jack want to stay, I'll say yes."

Jack stopped eating. "Oh, Mother——"

Abby interrupted; a change of subject seemed called for. She had figured out a plan. "Father, can't Jack and I go riding this afternoon? The wind's in the north, that means it will stay clear. We might go down to Mr. Lum's. Jack says he likes to ride horseback."

"All right, Abby, and on the way you can carry a message to Browning for me. I forgot to tell him this morning that I'm going to take a load of hogs to Olympia day after tomorrow. If he has some ready to go, I'll take them along. I saw by the paper that the *Eliza Anderson* is going to Victoria on Thursday and that there is a market for hogs, now, at a good price. Those Canadians use lots of bacon."

Aunt Ellen gasped. "Who is this Eliza Anderson? Sounds queer for a woman to be driving hogs to market."

Even Mother had to laugh. Father answered. "That's the name of a steamer, Ellen. Olympia, our capital, you know, is at the south end of Puget Sound. Victoria is up north on the straits, across from Port Townsend. Victoria is the capital city of Vancouver Island and British Columbia. The *Eliza Anderson* has a good trade running between the two places. She stops at Tacoma and Seattle, too, but they aren't important."

"I'd like to make that trip sometime," Uncle John said. "You know, Will, people back East have no idea what this country is like. Remember when we were boys and Polk was running for president? He said he'd fight to get the boundary clear up to Alaska and shut the British out. I know our neighbors said they'd never fight for a wilderness."

"Yes," Father answered. "The Army and some of the newspapers were yelling about 54° 40′ or fight. I wish my mother could see it out here; she was the one who got me interested. She heard Hall Kelley, from Boston, talk at Middlebury College once. Hall was crazy, I guess. He said this was a paradise. The way he talked, you'd think all you had to do was to stand at your back door and throw seeds out and you'd have all you could eat pretty quick. There's a lot of hard work, but I'm glad we came."

"I should think you would be," Uncle John said. "If you weren't yarning about those vegetables you raised, I'm here to stay."

Abby sighed. The conversation twisted like a garter snake and was as hard to drive as a pig. Out of the corner of her eye she could see Jack, his face as black as his hair.

He began to grumble. "Father! You said we could decide in the spring. I don't like being fenced in by trees; no smooth ground anywhere. I can't raise a garden or earn any money this winter. Don't you feel cooped up, Mother?"

Aunt Ellen looked worried. "I don't know. I wanted to come, but I do like the prairies, where you can see for miles. I don't like rain—but remember those hot winds back there. Then"—she looked at Uncle John—"there are other things besides weather to think about in choosing a home. Let's not spoil this good dinner; wait a few weeks."

"I want to earn some money, and I don't see any chance here," Jack insisted.

Henry had finished his dinner and was sitting by the fireplace picking his teeth with a splinter from the pile of kindling. He spoke so suddenly that the children jumped.

"Wait until you get pitch in your hair; then you'll want to stay."

"What does that mean?" Jack asked crossly.

"They say that when you stay here long enough to get pitch from the trees in your hair, you never want to leave," Mother told him. "They just mean that when you stay out West for a while, you like it."

"I won't like it." Jack spoke positively. "When we lived on the homestead in Kansas, we could go into Ness City sometimes and have fun. I'll bet nobody around here plays baseball." He jumped as Henry roared at him.

"Look out, young feller! You don't know what we do out here. Why, only last week we got the San Juan Islands tacked on to the United States because of a ball game."

"Wha-at do you mean?" Jack stammered.

Henry pulled his shoes off and stretched his feet out comfortably to the fire before he answered. "You see, there's been a lot of talk, ever since the boundary treaty was signed in forty-six about whether the San Juan Islands belonged to the United States or to England. Some rigamarole about a channel. So our government put it up to Emperor William of Germany to decide. Been making a peck of trouble. Well, last week there was a telegram tacked on the door of the newspaper office in Olympia telling about a ball game——"

"Olympia?" Jack interrupted.

"Yes, your uncle just told you that's the capital of Washington Territory, young feller. It's about thirty miles from here. Well, you see, the Olympia ball team was going up to Victoria to play. Did you hear him tell you about Victoria? It's on an island near the San Juan Islands, in Canada, so it's British. Tell you, this was a big ball game. Like I said, there was this telegram on the door, and this was what was on it: 'Emperor William has decided to let the result of the ball game in Victoria decide the international boundary question.' You can see, the Olympia boys felt a big responsibility. They played their best; they won; the Islands belong to the United States!"

Jack had been listening, looking more and more astonished. "Is that true, Uncle Will?" he asked. "Oh, excuse me, Henry."

Everybody laughed, even Henry, who tried to look fierce. "My stories are always true, young feller."

"It's true that the telegram was posted, and it's true that Emperor William gave the United States the decision," Father answered. "You can decide whether there was any connection."

While Henry was talking, Clara was rubbing the back of her neck. Now she began to cry.

"Why, Baby," Mother said, "whatever is the matter? Does your neck hurt? Come here."

Clara walked slowly, still rubbing under her curls. "This morning," she said, choking her sobs, "while I was waiting for Abby and Jack to tie the duck—oh, Abby, I forgot, I'm sorry. . . ." She began to cry harder.

"Go on," Abby said crossly.

"Well, I saw an old burned log that had pitch gum in it; and I got some, and began to chew it; then I knew I mustn't chew it in church, so I stuck it back under my hair, where I could get it again to chew. Now it's stuck and pulls my hair, and it won't come out!" She wailed louder than ever, and put her head on her mother's lap.

"There, there," Mother soothed her. "Abby, get my scissors." She cut enough hair to get the gum out. "Now, that will never show. Remember, Ellen, how we used to chew spruce gum? Well, you can't chew the fresh, so the children dig it out of old burned logs. Clara, when I saw you in church this morning, I thought that Abby had forgotten to wash your face; there was black on your mouth. Don't ever put gum in your hair again."

"What I want to know," said Father, "is the story about the duck."

While Abby was trying to think what would be the best way to explain, Jack surprised her by telling her father.

"That duck, Tilly, followed us up the trail to church, Uncle Will. I guess we didn't fasten his pen after we had been playing with him. Abby didn't want him to squawk during church, so I tied his bill shut."

"Jack was very clever, Father. He used my garter string and tied the bill and then sort of hobbled him. You know, you said if there was any more quacking during church, we'd eat Tilly. Father, I couldn't eat Tilly! It would choke me!" She started to gather up the dishes so the family wouldn't notice the tears.

"Can't blame the children, Will," Henry said. "I've been meaning to make that pen tight. Smart idea of yours, Jack."

"I used a hitch some cowboys taught me," Jack replied. "It's something like the way they tie the calves to be branded."

Abby saw that Father was laughing, so she knew he wasn't angry. There was a question she had been wanting to ask; this might be a good time. She went over to sit on his knee.

"Father, please, can I go to Olympia with you on this trip?"

"Abigail, don't tease."

"But you've always said that the reason I couldn't go to Olympia when you went was that there was nobody here to stay with Mother. And now there is. I want to see the school there, because maybe I'll get to go next year."

Uncle John turned to Father. "Remember, Will, I'm good for quite a good deal of work. Maybe I could help out so Abby could take the trip."

"We-ell," Father began to answer.

Abby interrupted. This seemed a fine place to let the matter stand, before he actually said no. After he once said that, it was hard to get him to change his mind. "I'll get at the dishes, Mother, so Jack and I can go on our ride. We'll want to get home before dark."

"Don't get too good, Abby," Father said with a smile. "I think you'd better start right away. It's several miles to Lum's, and I want you to stop at Browning's."

"Run along," Aunt Ellen said. "I'll help here, and you children can have a good time. Julia and I can just as well work while we visit."

Four

" 'Children,' " Jack muttered as they went out to saddle the horses.

"Riding is one of the things that I like best to do," Abby said as they went to the barn. "We'll take those two cayuses in the far stalls. Henry brought them from the Horse Heaven Country when he took a trip across the Cascades. He gentled them on the prairies over there. They're awful fast."

"They're awful skinny," Jack said, swinging the saddle over the back of one. The horse jumped to one side and tried to nip him. "Well, he's lively, all right."

"You can't ride a cayuse if you fatten him," Abby said. "They get too frisky. These won't buck—I hope—but they like to have their own way. They are good racers, too."

Jack stared when Abby sprang into a saddle like his. "I never saw a girl ride straddle before! So that's why you put on those funny baggy homespun trousers."

"Father asked Mother to make these trousers for me so I could help him in the woods. And he says it's safer to ride straight than sidewise. I don't have a girl's side-saddle and I don't want one. Most times I don't use any saddle at all." Abby touched her heels to the pony's flanks and was off on a run down the road. She called

61

back, "If you don't like the way I do things, stay home!"

He's an old fuss-budget, she thought. I'm tired trying to butter him up. He can go back to Kansas for all I care; there wouldn't be any fun in having him grouch around here.

"Hey, wait!" she heard him call, and after a bit she reined in her pony and let Jack catch up.

He grinned at her as he tried to ride alongside. "No use getting mad. I was just asking about things; I don't care what you wear."

"Look out, duck your head! There's a branch coming." At Abby's warning he crouched so the low branch from the tree only grazed him but didn't knock him off. "Watch where you're riding; you're not on your beloved Kansas prairies, you know," she said.

Jack laughed. "Say, I like you better when you're cross than when you try to be polite."

That made Abby laugh, too. "Well, I'm likely to take my company manners off if you try to boss me. Now watch where you're going, and I'll tell you about Claquato." She pointed to the ruins of an old building. "That's where they had a fort during the Indian scares. Just think, there were several families and some single men forted up in that place for months. There was a wedding and two babies were born and one little girl died."

"How did they manage to eat?"

"The men went out every day and tended to the crops, and then harvested them. Of course, they brought some cows up here. The men took turns standing guard."

"I'm glad things aren't like that now."

"Here is the Browning house; you wait, I'll be out in a minute." Abby threw her bridle over her horse's head, slid from the saddle, and ran up to the door. She was soon back and they were off. "I wish I hadn't been in such a hurry," she said. "Mr. Browning has some new dress goods in, just got a shipment from San Francisco. He has the best store between Portland and Olympia."

"Do you mean the only one?" Jack asked. "I certainly didn't see any stores along the way we came."

Abby pretended she didn't hear him. "Look at the old Davis house. Do you see how it is built? Two small log houses with a passage between and then an upstairs built over both to join them. But the stairs are in the passageway. I don't like it as well as ours. And see that enormous fir? That is called the immigrant's fir because the first settlers camped under it when they were traveling through. It's almost like a little house under it. You can see where they built fires and cooked. Now, let's get on the Military Road and off to Lum's."

"Why do you call it the Military Road? Are you expecting a war?"

"It was built for a military road. When President Grant was a lieutenant he was stationed out here and one of his projects was building a road from Vancouver to Fort Steilacoom."

"He didn't do a very good job," Jack grumbled. "Looks to me like they just cut down trees and rolled them to one side. I don't see how a wagon could go along this road. How do they get over the stumps?"

"Oh, people drive around them, or sometimes right over them. The wagon beds are built high so they can. This is lots better than the way the Hudson's Bay people used to travel. They went down the low road that's really a swamp. When it was rainy weather it was a swamp and they got stuck. When the river overflowed the horses had to swim."

"Kansas prairies are better," Jack said.

Abby started to argue, but saw that he was smiling. I believe he keeps saying that to tease me, she thought, and decided not to pay any attention.

"Next year there will be a railway right over there." She pointed across the Chehalis River. "But I'll always like to ride."

"What do I call this animal?" Jack asked. "I can't just say, 'Whoa, You!'"

"Yours is *Kloshe,* that means 'good,' and mine is *Skookum,* that's 'strong.' See, we're coming to a level stretch. Let's race."

Abby slapped Skookum's neck with a loose bridle, and he dashed off down the road. There couldn't be anything better than this, she was sure, galloping along a forest road with smells of evergreen around. She saw some bright red vine maple a little way off the road and decided to stop for some on their way back. Perhaps she would be riding along the road in a couple of days, going to Olympia. Only once had she been there when Father had taken the whole family so that Mother could do some shopping. That was when Clara was only a baby. There had been a traveling photographer there and Father had all their pictures taken to send to the grandmothers in Vermont. That would show that they didn't live in a wilderness.

While Clara was sleeping one afternoon, Mother had left her with Abby in the lobby of the Kneeland Hotel while she and Father went across to Mauerman's to buy some dress goods and kitchen things. Clara started to cry and a lady came in and rocked her and sang. She was a teacher, she told Abby. She seemed wonderful to Abby and from that time she wanted to be a teacher more than ever.

Thinking about Olympia and school made Abby so happy that she began to sing "Sweet Betsy from Pike." The road was narrower, so she slowed up and then remembered that she hadn't heard Jack behind her. She guessed he'd say she won the race, so she stopped Skookum and waited. She could neither hear nor see them, but they might be around one of the curves. Or had Jack been careless and let himself get brushed off?

Abby had just decided to turn around, when Jack and Kloshe came in sight. Her cousin was pulling at the reins and Kloshe was on a rampage. He jumped sidewise, and even seemed determined to go home. Abby laughed, but Jack's face was one black cloud.

"First time a girl ever beat me in a race! If I'd had a decent horse . . ."

"You don't know how to ride out here; it's not Kloshe's fault. Don't try to guide him in these ruts, he knows better than you. Just lean over his neck and whisper to him. Even then I might beat you; a girl is as good as a boy."

They rode on in a silence that made Abby unhappy. Everything had been so pleasant. Maybe Jack would like to hear her plans about school.

"One reason I want to go to Olympia Tuesday is that I think next year I can go to school there. I've been through the books here, and if I teach I must learn something more."

"I can't see why anyone wants to go to school," Jack said. "Mother used to be a teacher and she has the idea that someday I'll go back to Vermont to college. I don't worry about it, for I know we'll never have the money."

"What silly talk! Do you want to be plumb ignorant?"

"I can learn lots of things that they don't teach in school." Jack seemed to think that settled it.

"Probably, Jack, but not the right things."

"Well you sound like an old maid schoolteacher already."

Abby didn't care what he said, for a new idea had come to her. "If I could get some books, maybe your mother would teach me and then I could take the examinations next fall for some academy! And you could have classes with me! Mother doesn't want me to go to the school now they've moved it across the river. They've built a floating bridge, and she thinks it isn't safe."

"If you even suggest that I have lessons—sit by the fire like a sissy—I'll never help with anything you want, a pen for your pets, or anything."

Abby was glad that they were at the ferry so the argument stopped. They hailed Mr. Ready, who was on the bank, and he took them over. Jack helped wind the rope that connected with a stump on the other bank, and was in a good humor by the time they rode away. In a few minutes they were nearing Mr. Lum's cabin. Abby called to the pleasant-faced man loading wood on a wheelbarrow from a pile in the corner of the yard.

"Hello, Mr. Lum! Do you have time for visitors?"

"Of course. You children go on in and I'll be there in a few minutes."

They threw the reins over the horses' necks and started for the house. Suddenly Abby grinned. Might as well play a joke on Jack, she decided, he was so uppity about boys being so smart. She hadn't told him anything about Mr. Lum so she could surprise him.

Her cousin was close behind her, so when she opened the door, jumped to one side, and screamed, he was facing a huge cougar with lips drawn back in a snarl. The animal seemed ready to spring.

Jack was as frightened as she had hoped. He didn't stop to look, but dashed back into the yard, yelling, "Mr. Lum! There's a wildcat in your house!"

Abby stood on the little porch laughing. Mr. Lum shook his finger at her.

"Abby, you've been up to tricks! You didn't tell the boy that the cougar was stuffed."

"No, I didn't tell him you were a taxidermist. You see," Abby explained, still happy about her joke, "he thinks that boys are very much better than girls. I just wanted to find out whether he would protect me or run away!" She felt a little ashamed when Mr. Lum scolded her, and tried to make up for it by saying that they were very glad to have the Watsons visiting and hoped they'd settle in the Territory.

"That cougar," Mr. Lum told Jack, "was brought in by two boys from Lincoln Valley. They are about your age —maybe you'll bring me some animals someday."

Jack didn't answer, and Abby knew he was still cross. She wandered over to a glass case where Mr. Lum kept a beautiful wax doll. Abby felt too old to play with dolls, of course, but she could look at it and wipe her eyes without Jack's seeing her. Why couldn't she learn how to act, she wondered. Just when she was trying to make Jack happy; had planned this ride specially for him. Now he'd never want to stay. She'd been too smart about beating him in the race, too. She hadn't been listening to Mr. Lum, but now she heard Jack speaking in an excited way.

"You mean there are lots of animals around here and you buy them? I've shot coyotes back in Kansas; I'll bet I could learn how to get these animals."

"Ask Henry; he'll show you how to trap them," Mr. Lum said.

Abby moved nearer and pretended to look at birds and butterflies in a glass case.

Mr. Lum went on explaining. "I make my living this

way. I sell animals to museums back in the East. Ever hear of the Smithsonian? That's a large museum in Washington, D.C. They buy a good deal from me."

Jack was excited. "And you think I could earn some money? You might buy from me?"

"Sure. Bring me anything you get. If I can't use them, perhaps I can help you sell them. There's a bounty on a good many animals. Getting furs is what brought people to the Oregon Country in the first place, you know; some folks still make a living that way."

"You see, Mr. Lum"—Jack spoke slowly, as if talking was hard—"I need to earn some money. During the Battle of Vicksburg my father lost a leg and nearly died. He was in a hospital for months. Then when he was making his way back to Vermont, he found me in an old shed in the Blue Ridge Mountains. The place had been raided and my folks killed. Well, he took me home, so now I have real parents and I want to help them. So I have to live where I can earn money. I'm fifteen."

"I understand, Jack," Mr. Lum said.

Abby coughed. She thought she'd burst if she didn't get back into the conversation. "Mr. Lum can do lots of things, Jack. He is a surveyor, and mends watches and clocks, and he paints pictures, and plays the clarinet!"

Mr. Lum laughed. "After all those pretty words, Abby, I'll have to forgive you for scaring my guest."

"All right, Abby," Jack said, "I guess you put one over on me, but you would have been scared, too, if you hadn't known beforehand that it was a stuffed animal."

70

"Of course!" Abby agreed eagerly. "Even if I do know it, I feel shivery when I look at him."

Just then a loud neigh made them jump. "That's Skookum, I'll bet," Abby said. "He seems to know when it's time to go home. Come on, Jack. If we are late, I won't get to come the next time I ask."

"I want to come again too, and maybe I'll bring a cougar, Mr. Lum." Jack laughed, but he sounded like he meant it, Abby decided. "We'll likely stay out here till spring."

Abby made a face. "He doesn't like our country, Mr. Lum. He thinks Kansas is better."

"Well, Abby, give the boy time. He just got here yesterday. You need to learn patience."

"I like it better here than I did last night," Jack said. "Maybe all these woods are good for something if they have animals living in them."

Abby dug her heels into Skookum's flanks. "Let's gallop whenever we can. Mother won't like it if we are late."

A fog began to close in from the low ground before Jack and Abby reached the Claquato Hill. By the time they rode into the yard it was dark and they went directly to the barn. Henry came out and handed Jack a lantern.

"I never saw one like this before," Jack said as he took it.

"Probably not," Abby replied. "Henry invented this. He took an old tin can that axle grease came in, cut part of one side out, and soldered a candleholder in the bottom. Then he used some of the tin he cut out and soldered a handle at the back. See, it's safe, the candle won't fall out even when I tip it over, this way."

"Better hurry," Henry said. "Chores are all done, and it's time to eat. Bed your horses."

When they opened the kitchen door a smell of cooking greeted them. Abby sniffed. "Baked beans, that's what's in the Dutch oven. I saw them soaking last night."

Aunt Ellen shook her head. "Wrong guess. The beans are in that other kettle; I made some Boston brown bread and put it in the Dutch oven; may not be good, I never cooked on a fireplace before."

"Well, if it doesn't taste good, we can say it's because we are eating it on Sunday evening; it's a Saturday-night meal," Uncle John said.

"That's for Boston," Father said. "Out here in the West we eat what we want when we want it. We make our own traditions, or maybe we don't have any."

As she went upstairs to change to a dress, Abby looked back at the room. It couldn't be nicer, she thought. Uncle John was sitting by the fire, but he didn't look as sad as he had when they first came—why, that was only last night! If he could change that much in a day, by spring everything would be all right, she was certain.

The fireplace was filling the room with warmth and light. Mother and Aunt Ellen were hustling around, getting food on the table. Clara, as usual, was putting her corncob dolls to bed in the corner. Abby sighed.

72

If only things would stay that way, everybody happy.

Father came in from the bedroom, smoothing his hair. "Come, Abby, what are you gawking at? Aren't you going to eat with us? Better get washed up."

"I was thinking how happy the room looks. I wish it could stay that way, but when things are too nice, I always worry that something bad will happen."

Her uncle laughed. "That's your Conner Irish, Abby. You are afraid the Little People will feel that if things are too pleasant they should bring a little misfortune, just to make people careful."

"That's true," Henry said. "The Indians know there are bad spirits who listen when you brag, and——"

"Nonsense!" Mother banged the iron lid she was lifting down hard on the stone hearth. "People make their own trouble and then blame it on spirits."

"You know the old saying," Father said. " 'He who can't dance blames it on the floor.' "

"Come and eat," was Mother's reply.

Abby grinned as she hurried to get ready. Mother always got cross if folks talked as if they believed in superstitions.

Things kept on being pleasant all through supper. Everybody praised Aunt Ellen's cooking, and Uncle John and Jack were pleased. Mother said that she would have to make some of the brown bread the next time they had a big party; it would be something new. Then they had to tell the Watsons about the parties they had.

"Sometimes they are in Pearson's carpenter shop,"

Mother said. "That makes a good place for square dances when the lumber is stacked up and the shavings are off the floor. The sawdust makes the boards slick."

"People still talk about the 'Sanitation Ball' they had in Sixty-three, soon after we came," Father said. "That was to raise money for nursing the wounded soldiers. Each couple paid five dollars and they cleared $225 even though they had to pay fifty dollars gold for the musicians from Olympia."

"What do they usually do for music?" Uncle John asked.

"Father is thinking of his fiddle," Jack said.

Then Mother was really excited. "Did you bring your violin, John? You can play for us here at home. The Mills boys play for some of the dances, but they'll like to have your help. Remember how John called out square dances when we were all young in Vermont?"

There was a little silence and Abby began to worry for fear someone was getting sad thinking of old times.

"I went to the Sanitation Ball," she told Jack. "But I got sleepy—I was only two years old—and Mother wrapped me in a blanket and put me to sleep. I woke up and crawled into a pile of shavings then I crawled out on the floor with shavings stuck all over me."

"You must have looked cute," Jack said. "Of course you remember it?"

Abby didn't mind his teasing, for it got the others to talking again. Father told them that they always celebrated the Battle of New Orleans on January 8.

"Don't ask me why; I only know that it's a Claquato custom. It's a good time to get together; not much work we can do at home. We have a big dinner; the committee charges seventy-five cents and since everything is donated they have a tidy sum to buy something for the school, or to help pay for the teacher."

"I've been wondering about school," Aunt Ellen said.

"I'll get her mind off that!" Jack whispered to Abby. He pulled his stool over to the fireplace by Henry. "I got scared by a cougar this afternoon, Mother."

Aunt Ellen stopped clearing the table. "Oh, Jack, a cougar? Where? I was afraid when you children didn't get home before dark. . . ."

"This one wasn't dangerous, Mother. Just as we got to Mr. Lum's door Abby jumped back and yelled, 'Look out!' I could see a big beast inside, with its jaws open. I didn't know it was stuffed, so I ran to Mr. Lum in the yard, yelling for a gun. I left Abby to look out for herself."

"Abby," her mother scolded, "you ought to be ashamed. Of course Jack was scared. That animal is terrifying, anyway; I don't see how Mr. Lum stands it."

"Whatever does he keep it in his house for?" Aunt Ellen asked. She still seemed worried.

Jack was glad to explain. "He's a taxidermist. He sells animals back East and he's going to buy some from me. He says maybe I can get good furs, too. Do you think I can, Uncle Will?"

"Sure."

"I guess I'll forgive Abby for playing a trick on me, Aunt Julia, I'm so glad to have gone with her and found out how I can earn money."

Abby wondered why she had thought that Jack was a silent boy. He certainly could talk when he got started.

Henry squinted down the barrel of the gun he was cleaning. "Jack, I saw right away you were the kind of a boy I'd like to take on a hunting trip; you're big and strong and don't talk too much. Why don't we go down to the ocean and get some sea otter? Not as many as there used to be, but they pay big and they're easy to get."

"Now, Henry," Father said, "you promised me you'd help get the pigs to market and stay around till after the butchering. . . ."

"I know, William, I know," Henry answered. "We'll get the work in shape. I was only tellin' this young feller what we'd do someday."

"What are sea otter like?" Jack stammered with excitement. "Do you catch them with a line, or a net?"

"You shoot them," Abby told him.

"Nonsense!"

"She's right." Henry nodded. "The otters ride on top the waves. When they catch a fish they turn on their backs and float along eating. It's easy as pie to shoot 'em and pick 'em up when they drift in to shore."

"Is this——" Jack began, and then stopped.

Mother laughed. "I'm afraid that we've made you think all Henry's stories are made up. I've never seen them

76

get otter, but I think they do it that way. Speaking of easy as pie, who could eat a piece of Pope and Talbot pie?"

Uncle John was interested. "I'll take a chance on it, Julia. Is it some kind of new-fangled cooking?"

"No, it's another name for dried apple pie. Pope and Talbot are a logging company up Sound. They serve their men so much dried apple pie that the men named the pie after the company."

"If their pies were as good as those Julia makes, the men wouldn't grumble," Father said. "Abby, get the cups and some cream. What's that dried bean coffee steaming on the hearth for?"

After Abby had poured the coffee, she put her arms around her father's neck. "And speaking of p-i-e, what about p-i-g? Father, please, can't I go to Olympia with you?"

Father shook his head. "Mother and I talked it over this afternoon. You know about the work here, and where things are, so you should stay to help Uncle John with the chores. After John and Ellen have been here for a while and things aren't too rushed, maybe you can take a trip."

"I'll need you, too, Abigail," Mother said. "You remember the quilting party is this week; there'll be lots to do."

Father went on. "I think I'll take Jack with us. We'll need an extra hand to get the stock across on the Skookumchuck Ferry. I'm taking your calves and two more to sell, besides the pigs."

Abby didn't answer. She picked up the cream jug and started for the North Room. "I'll clear up, Mother, I guess everybody is through. I s'pose we'll have to get to bed early so we can get up early if there's so much work to do."

When she was safe in the North Room, Abby put the candle and cream down carefully before she began to cry. Just as she had said, things couldn't stay good the way they were before supper. Jack was going to have all the fun—he could go hunting, and go to Olympia, even if he was cross and grumbled. And she had worked and worked and nothing ever went right. All Father cared about was somebody to help with the work. And Mother let Clara play with her Queen Susan things. . . . Abby

stuffed her skirt in her mouth so her sobs wouldn't be heard. She was treated almost as bad as *Topsy* had been. Probably nobody loved her, either. But it was rather nice to feel like a heroine in a book. "Our heroine struggled on, although she was mistreated." Well, no, that sounded as if her parents beat her. Abby wiped her eyes. She felt better. She determined to be quiet and dignified and suffer in silence.

She found everyone in the other room hustling around, getting things in order. Jack and Henry were putting their whittling things away; Mother was undressing Clara; nobody noticed her. She sighed and took a book from the shelf and sat down at the table.

"Time for bed, Abby, don't start reading," Mother said.

"What's your book?" Uncle John asked.

"I thought I'd like to read one of Longfellow's poems before I try to sleep," Abby answered.

Jack snorted. "La-de-da," he said as he passed her.

Abby forgot her dignity and stuck her tongue at him. She gave her book one last look and put it away.

Father finished banking the fire and caught up with her as she started up the stairs. He kissed her and said to Aunt Ellen, "We chose a good name for our little girl. You know, 'Abigail' means 'her father's joy.'"

Abby hurried away; it was going to be hard to stay cross.

Mother had tucked Clara in bed. "Go to sleep right away, Abby," she said as she kissed her. "There are a lot of things that must be done tomorrow."

CHAPTER **Five**

Abby woke early. Usually she liked to hear the fog dripping from the trees that hung over the house. The roof was close to her head and the drip, drip made her feel calm and peaceful. This morning she was gloomy but couldn't think what was the trouble. Then as she became wider awake she remembered: tomorrow Jack would get to go to Olympia just because he was a boy; Aunt Ellen was sure to see that he went to college whether he wanted to go or not. Nobody really cared anything about her. What was the use of getting up? Abby pulled the blanket over her head.

Suddenly she remembered that Uncle John had told Jack that he must help her today. "Do everything that Abby tells you," was what he had said. What a wonderful chance to boss!

Abby heard Aunt Ellen and Uncle John talking quietly in the next room and then going down the stairs. She hurried into her clothes without waking Clara and went down to breakfast. Jack and his father were sitting by the fire waiting.

"Jack," Abby said, "you'll have enough time to get that pen finished for Tilly before breakfast is ready."

Jack started to grumble but his father said that was a

good idea and he'd better get to work, so he went out grumbling.

Abby and her uncle grinned at each other like a pair of conspirators. If Aunt Ellen and Uncle John would stay out West, Jack could go back to Kansas for all she cared, she thought.

As soon as breakfast was over Abby ordered Jack out to gather pine cones. "The wind last week blew a lot of them down. We'll put them in that big bin in the woodshed. Mother says we can't get too many; nothing beats pine cones for making a quick hot fire under the big iron kettle."

When the bin was nearly filled, they went out to the meadow. There were many stumps, some large ones, that were left when Father cut the trees. He burned the ground over before he sowed pasture seed and the fire had loosened the thick bark on the big stumps.

"We'll pull this bark off in long pieces," Abby said, "and pile them up. Henry will drive the oxcart out here and take it all to the shed. Mother never has too much bark; that's what she uses under the Dutch oven."

By the middle of the morning the fog was gone. The bright October sun made everything look gay. The sword ferns and bracken were turning a rusty brown that Abby thought would be a nice color for a dress. Beyond the meadow, the vine maple, scattered through the evergreens, looked like flames shooting up. That would be a nice color for a dress too. She stopped to admire the

81

Oregon grape that grew near the stumps. Usually the glossy leaves were a dark green, but now they had shades of red and gold shading into the green. She sighed. If she ever, ever got to go away to school, she knew the colors she would choose for dresses.

"Don't stop to gawk," Jack called. "You said we had to work fast to get everything done."

"Today is your day to work," Abby replied. "Your father said you had to help me before you go off on the trip, remember? I have to stop once in a while to look around; everything looks so pretty in the fall. Don't you think it's nice? Wouldn't you like to live here, always?" She stopped—she had forgotten again about talking so much about Jack's staying. Mother said it would make him stubborn.

"We-ell," her cousin answered, "I like some things here. Uncle Will said it was easy to trap for beaver, mink, and fresh-water otter, and that I could shoot bear and deer. I might like to cut down trees to clear things up so a person could see farther. And I guess it's more fun to gather bark and cut wood than to gather buffalo chips like we do in Kansas."

"Buffalo chips? Oh, yes, I know." Abby wrinkled her nose. "That's the manure the buffalo leave on the prairies. Well, I wouldn't like to pick them up, and I wouldn't want to eat the things cooked over them, either."

"That's silly." Jack stopped his work and glared at her. "They are dry, and you put them in a stove—we don't have to cook over a fireplace back in Kansas—and the food is as clean as can be. My mother is as good a cook as anyone, I'll have you know."

"You are the silly one." Abby knew she was talking too much, but she seemed unable to stop. "I know your mother is a good cook; I loved her supper last night. Come on, let's run a race. We'll each take a stump and see who can get the biggest pile of bark."

They worked silently for quite a while, then Abby said, "Of course, Jack, I hope you know that we are not obliged to cook over a fireplace; we have a stove. We like the fireplace better. Someday we'll get lots of things when the railroad goes from Kalama to the Sound. That might be next spring. Things will be sent from York State to San Francisco by railroad, then to Tacoma by boat, then here by rail. Just think, Olympia and Tacoma are on water that runs into the Pacific Ocean and goes all the way to China! Someday I'm going to travel everywhere on a big boat."

Jack didn't answer. Abby sighed and went on working. She didn't want to admit she was tired, for Jack was stripping off long pieces of bark and piling them up as if he had only begun to work. Abby decided he was working out his crossness with her. She was glad when they heard Mother ring the gong for them to come to dinner. It was fine to sit and rest while she ate a big bowl of mulligan stew and big slices of warm crusty bread.

"What's in here?" Uncle John asked.

"Venison and vegetables—potatoes, onions, carrots, turnips, cabbage, I guess," Abby told him.

"And you grew them all? This is the place for me."

Father had been talking to Henry about plans for a very early start the next morning. "And Abby, when you are through eating, ride up to the store. Your mother has some errands and I want you to tell Browning we'll be up there for his pigs by daylight tomorrow morning."

"All right, Father. Wait till you see the piles of bark we have out there. Jack is certainly a fast worker."

"He and I can haul it in," Henry said. "Then we'll get the wagon ready for those pigs."

At the store Nettie Browning waited on Abby. She weighed out some brown sugar and tea, and put down a package of cinnamon sticks. She carefully measured nine yards of unbleached muslin. "That's a good-looking cousin you have, Abby," she said as they put the things in the bag to sling over the saddle horn. "Is he going to stay out here long?"

"I don't know." Abby was surprised at how snappish her voice sounded. "The Watsons don't like the rain. I want the mail. Did the Portland paper come? Father may have time to read while he rests this evening. Don't forget to tell your father that they'll be here very early. I'll have to hurry now."

"That Nettie Browning!" Abby growled to herself as she rode home. "She's nosey. I suppose she'd think that Jack was good-looking, tall, and dark." Abby frowned; she didn't want to quarrel with Nettie; they'd always been such good friends. It was because she knew Nettie that Queen Susan had given her all those trinkets. The old Indian woman had kept two boxes in the Brownings' woodshed and showed her treasures to the two girls often. But there was no reason for Nettie to be so interested in Jack.

At home she found Mother and Aunt Ellen sitting by the fire, knitting and talking about old times when they were girls back in Vermont. Clara sat on the braided rug playing with her dolls. Abby pulled her stool to the fire and sat down to read the *Peterson's Magazine* Aunt Ellen had brought. First, she threw a small fir branch on the fire so there was more light in the room. Enough soft, fragrant smoke drifted into the room to be pleasant.

"This yarn is wonderfully soft, Julia," Aunt Ellen said. "You must have Mother's knack for spinning."

"Well, I have her spinning wheel and carder," Mother said. "But this yarn is made from very young sheep. One of our ewes had twin lambs last fall. We had to fuss all winter with raising them, but the work was worth while, for I found the yarn was extra soft when William sheared them last spring."

"This color is pretty, and different," Aunt Ellen said. "How did you get it?"

"Abby dyed that wool for her stockings herself. She picked salal berries, mashed them, and heated them to get the juice out. She strained it and boiled the yarn in it."

"It is the color of sunset over the mountain, Aunt Ellen." Abby had been listening with one ear.

"I worry about Abby's learning," Mother said. "For three years we had the best school north of the Columbia River. Miss Elizabeth Peebles, one of the Mercer girls, taught. Judge Jackson even sent two of his daughters to board at the Brownings' so they could go to the Claquato school."

"Then last year Miss Peebles got married," Abby told

her aunt. "Why she should get married when she could teach, I can't understand. Judge Mackintosh kept coming and coming to see her and at last she said she would marry him. I guess she was sorry for him. Nettie and I didn't like it at all."

"I'm mixed up. Was her name Peebles or Mercer or what?" Aunt Ellen asked. "It doesn't matter, since I suppose it is Mackintosh now."

Mother smiled. "Perhaps it did sound odd. Asa Mercer, the president of the university, thought there ought to be more nice girls in Washington Territory. So he went back to New England and arranged for their transportation. Everyone called them the Mercer girls."

"I remember; there was a piece about it in the Boston paper. Made quite a fuss. There were letters published saying the president ought to stop it some way."

"The girls were very nice. We've always been fortunate in our school; everyone is interested, and helps. When Mr. and Mrs. Davis gave the land and lumber for the church, nearly fifteen years ago, they said it must be used for a school for six years. So that and the upstairs in the courthouse have made good places for the school."

Uncle John came in while they were talking. "Courthouse? In your village?" he asked.

"Yes, didn't Will show it to you? Claquato has been the county seat of Lewis County for nearly thirty years. Now they are moving it to Saundersville, down on the flats, because the railroad is going through there. And our school is going to be across the river. I don't want the children going there, for last year the floating bridge they went on was washed away."

"Mother, you aren't making Claquato sound like a nice place to live. Don't worry about the school being across the river; I've gone as far as they teach, anyway. Miss Peebles gave me history, and even some algebra. I should go away. That's why I hoped——" Abby stopped abruptly. There she was again, talking about the Watsons' staying.

Aunt Ellen smiled at her. "I was thinking, Julia, that if we are here until next spring I might teach Abby. I brought some books, hoping Jack would be interested. But he talks all the time about getting work."

Abby jumped up and hugged her aunt. "Will you really give me lessons, Aunt Ellen? I must learn lots so I can be a teacher, like Grandmother Conner, because I'm named for her. She says that whenever she writes, but I want to be a teacher, anyway. That's why I hope you and Uncle John decide to live here, so I can go away. Father won't let me go and leave Mother alone." Abby felt her face getting hot; that didn't sound the way she meant it. "Of course, you know that I want you to live here because I like you, not just so you'll help me."

Aunt Ellen smiled again. "That's all right, Abby. We all have selfish reasons, but we aren't all so honest in saying so."

"And you will teach me?"

"I'd like to, very much."

Abby took Clara's hand and made her dance around.

Clara didn't know what it was about, but she always wanted to do what Abby did.

"If you are rested, Abby, you'd better get at your chores," Mother said. "It's getting dark. Be sure to put your special chickens in their coop and shut it tight, so the rats can't get in. I noticed that they are getting the notion of flying; you'll have to put them in another pen soon, or they'll roost in the trees."

As she got ready to go out, Abby began to make plans about her special chickens, as Mother called them. An old hen had stolen her nest late in August and Abby found the chicks as they were hatching. Mother said they could be hers if she wanted to take care of them. Mrs. Mills at "Our House" where the stage stopped to change horses, often needed extra chickens or eggs.

I can save my chicken money for clothes, Abby decided. Every little bit helps. Then if the Watsons stay out here, and I get to go away to school . . . She giggled. Counting my chickens before they are sold!

Abby made good resolutions while she dashed around doing her work outdoors. She determined not to mention school, going to Olympia, or anything like that for at least a month. She would do her work, keep Mother in a good humor, find things to make Aunt Ellen happy, not grumble when Jack had more good times—she could almost feel her wings sprouting under the heavy work jacket she wore. If she could only remember not to talk about it all the time. In spite of Father's quoting from Shakespeare or somebody about keeping quiet, Abby knew she would forget and spoil things by talking. She decided to practice that very evening.

Nobody seemed inclined to talk at supper; it was a quick and silent meal. When they finished, Father said everyone should turn in and get some sleep; that he and Henry had everything ready for a very early start.

"If you are going to carry the hogs loose in the wagon, you'd better plan on putting the chicken coop up by the dashboard in front," Henry advised. "I made a good coop out of small cedar branches, but those hogs could soon smash it."

Father agreed. "Some of the money we get for the chickens is yours, Abby. Any errands I should spend it on?"

Abby shook her head. "I am saving all my money. There may be a special use for it next year." She went quickly upstairs before there were any questions asked her. It was fun to be mysterious; she hoped Jack was puzzled.

Clara was already asleep, but Abby turned and wiggled; there was so much to think about she couldn't sleep. After all, not going to school regularly wouldn't be bad, not as long as she could study with Aunt Ellen. No girls her own age would be in school next year; all the big girls were thinking about getting married.

Her first new dress would be blue silk, she decided. One with flounces, like that picture in Aunt Ellen's magazine, would be nice, but Mother might say that it was for an older girl. Mother couldn't realize that Abby was pretty old, thirteen this winter. Mary Jane Mills was married when she was fourteen. Most girls Abby knew didn't want to teach, or go around the world.

A plume on a hat would be beautiful, but it wouldn't last long in the rain. Better take Mr. Lum's offer. He said he would cure the breast of a pheasant; she could put it on a brown velvet toque. She'd get a brown velvet dress to travel in.

She yawned, and was dozing off when a noise roused her. At first she thought it was Uncle John snoring, then she realized that it was her little chickens fussing. The coop was under her tiny window so she could hear. Nobody else was stirring. Botheration! She might as well see what the trouble was. If anything happened to the chickens—that much less money.

In the dark she felt for the heavy robe and moccasins by her bed and slipped them on. She crept down the stairs and out the door. The moon was shining so brightly that she could see her way, but she turned the corner so rapidly that she bumped into Jack, who was ahead of her.

"Sh-h," he whispered. "Let's see what's after your chickens. Look!" They had come close enough so they could see a skunk slipping between the crisscrossed saplings. He had a chicken in his mouth.

Abby had not noticed what Jack was carrying, so she jumped as an arrow swished through the air. It caught the skunk in the head and killed him so quickly he had no time to throw out his defensive smell.

"Oh, Jack, how did you do that?" Abby whispered through chattering teeth; she was both scared and cold.

"That's nothing." Jack got another arrow ready and walked over to be sure the skunk was dead. "I happened to have these out; I was showing them to Henry last night. I told him that arrows were better than shots; don't make so much noise. Say! do you suppose we could sell that skunk?"

"Sure you can; you hit him right in the head and the skin won't be broken at all."

"Well, you run back to bed; we'll see about him in the morning. I'll have to risk leaving him here tonight. If I touch him, Henry won't want me in the same room!"

Abby giggled. "I was figuring last night how much money I'd make on these chickens when they were grown, so I forgot to put the boards tight in front of the coop."

"I'll do it." Jack slid the boards close to the old hen that was muttering reassuringly to her chickens. "Listen," he whispered and Abby turned back. "We'll divide the money if we sell that skunk; it was your chicken that baited him. And, Abby . . . I'm sorry you can't go with us tomorrow—or is it today?"

He walked away before she could answer, but what he had said made her happy; sounded just like they were partners. Maybe he'd forget their quarrel in the woods. She crept noiselessly to bed and snuggled to Clara to get warm. She hoped the skunk had taken only one chicken.

Abby found it hard to believe that morning had come when she heard Mother whisper, "Get up quietly, Abby, don't wake Clara. We must hurry with breakfast; Father wants to start as soon as he has finished eating."

The day was cold and gloomy. Aunt Ellen was shivering, with a heavy shawl around her, when she came to breakfast. "I declare," she said, "I never thought there could be fog like this. I can't see ten feet from the door. Will, you can't drive in this; it isn't safe."

Father chuckled. "Nothing to it. The horses know their way, I just let them go. They have to see only as far as their feet—there's only one road. But, shucks, this isn't a bad fog. The worst one I ever saw was when Henry and I were shingling the barn. We thought it was taking us a long time, and sure enough, when the sun came out we found we had shingled over six feet of fog!"

Aunt Ellen started to laugh but she sniffed as Jack sat down at the table. "Jack, it's you. I've been thinking for several minutes that I smelled something disagreeable. Where have you been?"

Abby interrupted. "Oh, Aunt Ellen, you should have seen what Jack did last night. We both heard a noise out in the yard near the chicken pen. We went out and there was a skunk stealing my little chickens. Jack shot it with his bow and arrow; killed it, first shot. I don't think it smells—much."

"Where is it now?" Uncle John asked.

"Why—I took it into the woods and I've been skinning it——" Jack began.

Mother stopped him. "Come here. You take this pan of hot water and this soap and go out to the barn and wash up. I put carbolic acid in that soap when I made it last spring; it will take one smell away. Throw all those clothes out in the yard and put on some clean ones."

"Go fast," Father said. "We're starting soon."

Abby felt they were making too much fuss about a little smell. "Jack wants to sell the skin to Mr. Lum," she explained. "I think he was very smart to kill the skunk so quietly that none of you heard him."

When Jack came back he ate in a hurry, and in a few minutes was out in the yard helping the men.

They soon had the wagon loaded with squealing pigs.

The chickens squawked as Henry tied their feet together and put them into the pen he had made. Father put it in front of the seat and he and Jack climbed up while Henry went to get Skookum.

Abby stood by the front wheel. Perhaps Father would take a hint. "Might need an extra hand as far as the ferry, getting the stock across, don't you think?"

"Guess we'll manage," he answered.

Abby threw her good resolutions out in the brush. "All right, but if any of those calves are drowned crossing the river, it had better not be mine. I need that money." She ran back into the house and banged the door. She was too cross to cry. Jack made her furious too. He hadn't spoken to her all morning; now he sat up on that seat like he was running the whole business. She wasn't going to stand out there and wave good-by to them, that was sure. She poured a cup of coffee and spread jam on a thick slice of bread.

When the others came in, she asked, "Mother, if I hustle through my chores, may I go for a ride this morning? When the fog clears."

Her mother thought a minute. "Yes, I'll tell you what. With this early start you'll be through your work by the middle of the morning. I'd like to have you take that cloth you bought yesterday to Mrs. Washington and ask her to sew it on her machine. It's the lining for my new quilt. If you go directly there, you can get back early so you can help Uncle John with the chores before dark."

Uncle John, who had been sitting near her drinking a

cup of coffee, laughed. "It's the other way around, Julia, I help her. She certainly knows how to run things. Too bad she wasn't a boy. You ought to marry a farmer when you grow up, Abby."

"I'm not going to get married." Abby spoke through a mouthful of bread and jam. "I'm going to be a teacher, and when I get enough money I'll travel all over the world."

"Who is Mrs. Washington?" Aunt Ellen asked.

"The Washingtons live down the river, near what they call 'Cochran's Landing,'" Mother answered. "He was a free Negro, half white, who came from Missouri with a white couple who had adopted him. They died several years ago and later he married a widow with one child. She has some colored blood, I understand. They are wonderful neighbors, always helping someone. They have the only sewing machine in the county, I believe. It certainly saves time."

Abby dashed out the door, determined that she would have the chores done quick as you could shake a stick. She helped Uncle John with the milking and he carried the pails of foamy milk to the North Room to strain. Abby put hay in the stalls and took the cows for a drink at their well in the barnyard; then she opened the gate so they could go down the lane to the pasture. She took food to the pets, but didn't stop to play with them; fed the chickens and geese and went to the house.

"Everything is done, Mother. May I go?"

"There's your churning . . . Never mind, go on, we'll

manage. I'm glad it's clear weather so the men will have a good day to come home; I'm always afraid of storms this time of year. Take these lengths of cloth and this thread and ask Mrs. Washington to please stitch them together for me. Perhaps there will be some work you can do for her."

"Yes, Mother." Abby had been pulling on her best hood and her cape. The loose trousers she wore to work would be fine for riding. She fastened her cape tight and ran out to saddle Kloshe.

As she rode back toward the house, her mother called to her to wait. Abby groaned. "I hope she hasn't decided that I must do some more work before I go."

However, her mother just handed her a cloth bag. "There's no use sending Mrs. Washington any vegetables or fruit. They have such a wonderful garden that they give truck away. But this is some salt-rising bread that your aunt made yesterday; it's right tasty."

Abby fastened it to her saddle, along with the roll of goods, and galloped down the trail. When she reached the road she went more slowly; the morning was beautiful and she liked to see the view over the valleys. The hills toward the ocean were deep purple blue, but directly across the river the woods were bright with colors. At the ruins of the old fort she reined Kloshe. It had been built on a high place so that the guards could see for miles around. Abby always thought that she would like to have a house there.

A big flock of birds were chattering while they feasted

on madroña berries. Going South, Abby thought, and they travel so easily and don't have to worry about clothes. Chipmunks whisked up and down trees gathering seeds from the fir cones. The quiet of the morning was broken by the clatter of wheels and loud calls of "Whoa! Whoa!" What luck! The stage was arriving. She rode slowly toward the Mills'; she liked to watch the passengers and imagine where they came from. Three men, all dressed in city clothes, got out and stretched. Government men, going to Olympia, Abby thought, trying not to stare.

When Mrs. Mills opened the door for them she saw Abby. "Please, Abby, come here!" she called, and went back into the house.

Abby rode Kloshe nearer and threw the reins over a picket of the fence. Kane Mills and the stage driver were taking the horses to the barn to change them for fresh ones.

She went in the back door to the kitchen and found Mrs. Mills in a fret.

"You can help, Abigail, for a fact. Wash your hands and help me dish up. I'm alone today and of course the stage came early. Lucky I have things cooked from Sunday dinner. Those men won't wait a minute, you know. Soon as that driver shovels a little food in him, he'll want to go."

Abby quickly put big platters of ham and roast chicken on the table, then went back for mashed potatoes and a bowl of dried corn and beans. Mrs. Mills handed her a plate of bread and put a pound of butter on a gold-edged glass plate. Pickles and jam and apple butter were already on the table.

While Mrs. Mills cut pie and cake, Abby kept filling the cups with coffee. She noticed the men didn't talk much, but they piled food on their plates. Being dressed up and looking important certainly didn't hurt their appetites.

"Good dinner," one of the men said. "I'm glad we stopped here to eat; hope we can get to Olympia soon. We ought to give this young lady something to show we appreciate her serving us so quickly. Here's two bits."

The other men agreed and each gave Abby a quarter. She was so surprised that she could only stammer her thanks before they were gone. Mrs. Mills was clearing the table as the stage drove off with a great clatter. Abby offered her the money.

"Of course I won't take it, child, it's yours." She took the money the men had given her from her pocket and handed another quarter to Abby. "Yes, take this. If you hadn't helped me the men would have been impatient; they were in a rush. Now, sit down and we'll have a bite."

"I should hurry, Mrs. Mills. Father has gone to Olympia and I must get home to help Uncle John with the chores. I have to go clear to the Washingtons' with this sewing."

"Well, let your pony rest, and he can go faster. I want you to try this cake. I used a new receipt. First, eat some ham—what about a chicken leg?"

Everybody said Mrs. Mills was one of the best cooks in the county; the cake was delicious and Abby asked for the receipt. She stayed quite a while; Mrs. Mills talked like they were two women eating and visiting.

When she reached the Military Road, Abby made good time. There were places along the Flats where she could gallop in spite of the mud. On the low places the fog was already rising. That might mean that tomorrow would be clear, but tonight, dark would come very early.

"Hurry, Kloshe," she urged. "I've dawdled and I mustn't be late getting home."

She had tied her money in her handkerchief and put it safely inside the neck of her waist. A dollar! That would buy a hat next year when she went away.

"I can't help thinking about going to school, but I won't say it out loud," she promised herself.

Fortunately the Washingtons were home and not very busy. When Abby explained her errand, Mr. Washington took the bundle and brought out his long shears.

"I'd like to do the sewing," he said. "You know I learned to tailor when I lived in Missouri. Someday I'll make a dress for you."

"Oh, really? I'm saving my money for when——" Abby stopped, but nobody seemed to notice. Mr. Washington was at the machine and his wife was putting things on the table.

"Sit up and have something to eat, Abby," she said.

"I'm not hungry, really, Mrs. Washington. The stage

was at the Mills' when I went by, and I stopped to help Mrs. Mills, and ate, too. Mother will be worried if I'm late."

"Well, you might as well eat a little while George does the sewing; it won't take any longer." She called to her son, who was in the yard. "Stacey! Abby might like to see those pictures you brought from Victoria."

Abby knew that Stacey, a year younger than she, had gone to school in Victoria, but in the spring he had come to live with his mother and stepfather.

"Which school do you like best?" she asked.

He brought the pictures and laid them on the table and sat down before he answered. "I'm glad to live at home, but school was nicer in Victoria. Down in that little school by the gravel pit, some of the boys make fun of me because I have Negro blood. I had to knock a few of them down. Father said I shouldn't fight; it wouldn't settle anything, but I got so mad I forgot. Anyway, the boys are more friendly now because they want me to help them out on Friday afternoons."

Abby stopped looking at the pictures. "What do you do?"

"You see, the teacher likes to have singing and recitations on Friday afternoon. Most of the boys don't like to learn poems. I do, and I learned so many in Victoria that I can go on and on. So the boys try to have me called on first, and then I recite so long that there is no time for them."

Abby laughed. "I wish I had time to hear you; I like

101

poems. Do you like to read? I have four books—*Little Women, Uncle Tom's Cabin, Old-fashioned Girl,* and *Ivanhoe.* These pictures are interesting; the big houses are wonderful. Someday I wish you'd tell me all about Victoria, and about California, where you lived before. When I grow up, I'm going to travel."

"I hope you can, Abby," Mr. Washington said, handing her the sewing, "but now I'm afraid you must travel home. You have a long way to go, and I don't want to think of you out after dark. Next time, come early."

Abby bundled up quickly, for she saw it was late. "I'll bring my cousin Jack over someday; he and his folks are visiting us. And Stacey, you come over. Jack doesn't like poems, I'm afraid, but he likes boys." She thanked them again and ran out to Kloshe.

The fog was so thick by the time she reached the Hill Road that she couldn't gallop; her pony might stumble in the deep ruts. Darkness had come before she reached home. She threw the bridle over Kloshe's neck and ran into the house.

"Abby!" Mother exclaimed. "Where have you been? What will your father say? We have been so worried. I thought I might have to start out looking for you. You know your father said for you to help here at home, and

you should have been here before dark. Go right out now and help your uncle. No, don't stop to explain, you can tell about it later."

Things never stay right, Abby thought. She had enjoyed the day, but now everything was spoiled. She wished she could get on Kloshe and ride away and never come back. Of course, she loved Mother, even if she was unreasonable, but she couldn't stand everything.

Abby took the saddle and bridle from Kloshe and wiped her eyes on his mane. She tucked her face in her pony's warm neck and he nuzzled her hand as if he was sorry for her. She felt Prince at her side and patted him. Dogs and horses, she thought, are really better than human beings.

"I can finish the milking, Abby," her uncle called. "You throw the hay down and put grain in the feed boxes. I fed the poultry."

Very soon Abby and Uncle John had everything finished and went in the house. As she blew out the candle in the lantern she heard Aunt Ellen say, in a low voice, "I'm sure there is some explanation, Julia; Abby is such a responsible child."

Funny, having something nice said made her want to cry. It was easier not to cry when she was mad. She took a long time to hang up her things and to pull off her muddy shoes. Then she went slowly upstairs to change her trousers for a dress and to put on clean stockings and her moccasins. Maybe if she was long enough she wouldn't have to sit at the table with the others.

Finally Mother called, "Come, Abby, supper is ready. What's keeping you? We want to hear about your adventures."

Abby hurried then, and as they sat down at the table Mother said, "Probably something happened that you couldn't help."

She knew that was as near as Mother would ever come to say she was sorry for scolding, so she began to talk, fast. "Here's the quilt lining, Mother. Mr. Washington sewed it himself. Did you know he makes all of Stacey's clothes, and of course his own, and even some of Mrs. Washington's? He's very clever. Here are some needles that Mrs. Washington sent. A friend in Portland gave her a lot of needles and thread."

"Good," Mother said. "Now we can use new ones for the quilting. Everybody sit down before supper gets cold."

While they ate, Abby told why she had been late. "I'm afraid I didn't hurry enough when I started. Everything was so beautiful this morning I couldn't go fast. I stopped at the old fort ruins and planned how I could have a house there that looked clear over to the hills between us and the ocean."

Uncle John laughed but Mother frowned. "That was a waste of time," she said.

"Then, before I rode on I saw the stage coming and I watched the people getting out. Mrs. Mills saw me and asked me to help her because she was alone today and the stage driver was early because they were rushing to

Olympia. I think it was government men that were on the stage." She stopped to eat.

"We-ell," Mother said, "of course Mrs. Mills is always very kind about helping other people . . ."

"So I helped her hustle things on the table. My, those men could get on the outside of a lot of food, even if they were all dressed up and looked important. Then Mrs. Mills wanted me to try her cake. She had a new receipt. I really didn't waste a minute at the Washingtons'; as soon as the sewing was finished I started back. But the fog was thick. . . ."

Mother nodded. "I guess you couldn't have done much different. It wasn't that I wanted you here to work; I was worried about your being out after dark. It was about two years ago that a cougar jumped down on some children coming home from school late."

"But they were walking, Mother. Riding Kloshe is safe. And I almost forgot to tell you—those men each gave me two bits, and Mrs. Mills gave me another." She shook them out on the table.

"Let me play with them, Abby," Clara said.

"Only a few minutes; then they go up in my Queen Susan box."

"I think that was very nice, Abby," Uncle John said. "I'm sure you'll find something wise to spend your money on."

"Yes," Mother said, "she doesn't have very many chances to buy things." She sighed. "I hoped this fog meant that we'd have clear weather tomorrow; so if the men made good time going they would come right back. But I looked out a few minutes ago and the wind has shifted to the south. Can't tell."

Abby thought there was no use worrying ahead about the weather. Anyway, she was feeling more cheerful; things had turned out fine after all. But the day had certainly been a seesaw. First she had been glum when Father wouldn't let her ride even a little way. Then she was up in the air with happiness when she had a good ride and earned some money. Then, splang, down on the ground when Mother scolded. Now she was up, she was going to bed before anything else happened.

Six

Clara was the only one who slept late the next morning. Abby woke with a jump when a limb hit the roof and slid off against her little window. She found the others downstairs, Mother and Aunt Ellen looking out the window every few minutes and worrying about the men driving home. A gale was blowing, and the rain came down in sheets, Mother said. Abby thought it was more like someone turning over enormous tubs of water high in the sky.

The chores took longer, for the wind was so strong that Uncle John could hardly keep his balance. Abby made him do the inside chores; he helped milk and then cleaned the stalls while Abby took the cows for water and turned them out for pasture. She laughed because they looked so forlorn when she shut the gate. "Never mind," she told them, "it isn't cold, and fresh air is good for you. Find some grass."

The few pigs that were left grabbed the corn greedily and chewed the cobs as well as the grain. Abby fed the turkeys and left them in the shed.

The clock was striking eleven when the two "hired men" came into the house after finishing the morning's work.

"We'd better rest and then start on the evening work right after dinner," Uncle John said. "Otherwise we'll not get through before dark."

Dinner was a glum meal. Gusts of wind blew branches off the trees, and Aunt Ellen jumped whenever they hit the house. Mother worried about the men, although Abby reminded her that Father said he might stay an extra day in Olympia.

"We don't know that he did," Mother snapped.

Abby realized that things might go better if she kept quiet and didn't talk too much about anything. When folks were in a fret they often said things they didn't mean, and when cross things were said they were hard to forget.

The work went better in the afternoon, and before dark Abby sent her uncle into the house and she did the last chores, mostly feeding her pets. She didn't like to look at the bear cub; he was getting so big she knew that before long she must take him into the forest. The tall trees behind the house looked like children playing tag as they tossed their branches against each other. Abby picked up an armful of fir twigs with cones on them and carried them into the house.

"There, Uncle John, that's one good thing the wind did —broke these little branches off for us," she said, throwing them down near the fireplace. "We can throw one on the fire once in a while; it makes the room light and cheerful and smells nice." She took off her heavy cape and shook it; water from it splattered into the fire.

"Abby, be careful, I have things cooking there."

"I'm sorry, Mother." She hung her things away, soberly.

"Probably the men won't get home even tomorrow," Mother said. "The wind will blow trees down across the road, and by the time those are cut and dragged off the road—I don't know when they'll get here. I wish they had ridden horseback instead of taking the wagon; it's faster and they could get through more easily."

"Will had to take the wagon to carry the pigs, Julia," Uncle John reminded her. He chuckled. "You can't drive pigs; they run from one side of the road to the other; never seem to know what they want. Will said they changed their minds as often as women, never know what they'll do!"

Abby laughed, but her mother and aunt didn't.

"I'm glad this house is solid. I never heard such a terrible wind," Aunt Ellen said.

"Blows just as hard as this in Kansas." Uncle John sounded stubborn.

"I don't like wind anywhere, but it's worse in the forest," Aunt Ellen insisted. "On prairies there's nothing to blow against the house. This is dangerous."

"That's right," he answered, "but I believe I remember a tornado that took house and all from a homestead near us."

"John, please don't argue," Aunt Ellen said.

"We're having supper so early we'd have time to play

110

school tonight. Then we'd forget the wind." Abby thought that was a good suggestion.

"Oh, not tonight, Abby," her aunt answered. "I'm as nervous as a witch, I couldn't teach you anything." She stooped to take the lid from a kettle and a gust of wind came down the chimney and scattered ashes and smoke into the room. "There, see what I mean?"

"I think you're right, Abby. If we are busy we won't hear the wind." Uncle John took the turkey wing and brushed the hearth. "After supper you get your slate and I'll give you spelling and some arithmetic problems. I know as much about that as your aunt does. I can't help you parse sentences, but that's plumb foolishness, anyway."

Abby thought that Aunt Ellen should stop grumbling and be happy to hear Uncle John joke. But probably she was worried, really.

"Abby," Clara said, "I want to play with your Queen Susan box."

"Get it for her, Abby," Mother said. "She's been shut up in the house all day. The storm makes her nervous, like the rest of us."

"Oh, Mother, she has other things . . . Well, all right, but you'd better be very careful, Clara. If you lose a single one I won't ever let you play with them again."

Aunt Ellen stopped setting the table. "Well, who on earth is Queen Susan?"

"She was the wife of the chief of the Chehalis Indians," Abby explained. "After he died, she married an Indian slave. The tribe drove her out, for they thought she had disgraced herself and them, too. She put two trunks full of clothes and trinkets in the Brownings' shed. Sometimes she came back to look at them and she would let us girls look at them and she gave us a few things. Then, not long before she died, I found her in the woods with a sprained ankle. She had gone to pick berries. I helped her here to our house and Mother took care of her. So she gave me this box of beads and things. It's really my greatest treasure, and I don't like Clara playing with it very much."

"Abby was very good taking care of old Susan," Mother said. "I was glad she was grateful."

Uncle John held up a long string of blue beads. "Where do you suppose she got these?"

"The Hudson's Bay people used them for trading," Abby answered. "See, they are on a common string, with knots between each two beads. They cut off the number that they wanted to trade for fish or furs or whatever the Indians brought. Henry says these copper bracelets came from Montreal; the *voyageurs* traded them for beaver and otter."

"Time for supper," Mother said.

Abby looked at the table. Even if Mother was worried, she always cooked good meals. Here was hot bread, and venison with brown gravy, and pie for dessert. The little stove had been busy all day, for Mother and Aunt Ellen had baked pies and cakes ready for the quilting on Friday. Abby was hungry and ate and ate.

112

"You're going to be too stuffed to spell, Abby," Uncle John said. "Your cheeks look like two red apples."

Later she felt her cheeks getting red when he bragged about how good she was in arithmetic. Before they knew it, Mother and Aunt Ellen were listening and spelling some hard words that Abby missed. After Clara had carefully put away the Queen Susan things, they let her feel important by spelling "cat" and "dog."

Suddenly Mother went to the door. "Listen, I don't believe the wind is blowing." She opened the door, and sure enough, everything was quiet and the stars were shining.

"Bad storms often stop quick," Mother said. "I'm going to try to think that the folks didn't start back today. If tomorrow is clear, they'll make it through by evening. Let's get to bed; there's lots to do tomorrow. I'm going to roast a ham in the fireplace. Abby, you'll have to get two old hens ready for Aunt Ellen to make chicken pies. I'm making crullers on the little stove; it saves stooping."

"Sure takes a lot to feed these female famine sufferers that are coming Friday," Uncle John said. "How long has it been since they've had anything to eat?"

The way the two women laughed made Abby think that the weather had cleared up inside the house as well as outdoors. She was happy when Mother kissed her and said that she had been a big help that day; that Father would be proud when he heard all she had done.

"I'm glad, Mother, but he won't expect me to stay home all my life, will he?"

"Oh, Abby, don't start that, it's bedtime."

"Don't worry, Abby." Uncle John spoke up quickly. "I'm going to be able to help your father. You must have a chance at school if that's what you want."

"But, John," Aunt Ellen began, "I'm not certain——"

"Listen, Ellen, we don't know anything about this country. We've been here only a few days. You think they always have storms."

"We don't, Aunt Ellen . . ." Abby began.

"I'm sleepy," Clara whined.

"We all are," Mother said. "Take her to bed, Abby."

Abby boosted Clara ahead of her up the stairs, still listening to the others.

"As for Jack," she heard her uncle say, "like as not he'll come home from this trip dead set on staying out here."

Uncle John could think of the nicest things to say, Abby decided. She placed her good resolutions where she could put them on when she dressed the next morning. Mother would see, she wouldn't have a thing to complain about tomorrow!

The day started well, for Abby woke early and was soon downstairs. A peek out the door showed that everything was clear—the sky, the stars, the big full moon just setting in the west. The sharp, frosty smell of the air pushed a person to work.

Inside, too, things were bright. Uncle John sat in the corner by the fire, in a chair that he called his. "Haven't had a fireplace since I left New England," he told Abby.

"No wood to waste in a fireplace in Western Kansas, you know."

Aunt Ellen didn't pay any attention to that remark. She was dishing big bowls of hominy grits that had cooked all night in an iron kettle over the coals. Mother poured coffee and brought in pitchers of cream and creamy milk from the North Room. Abby turned the bacon that was sizzling in a spider on the hearth, then lifted the meat and slid the eggs she had broken into a bowl into the hot grease.

While they ate, Mother planned the day. "You get at the chores as soon as it's light, Abby. Later you can help here in the house. Everything must be shining-clean for the quilting tomorrow. If I had known that Will was going to make the Olympia trip this week, I might not have planned the party. But it will give Ellen a chance to get acquainted with the neighbors first thing." She looked anxiously around. "They'll have to take the house as they find it."

"Well, from all I've seen and heard they won't starve to death, anyway," Uncle John said.

Abby gave him a little hug as she went to pour fresh coffee. Were all uncles that nice? If they were, she wished she had a dozen. Last night he had taken everybody's mind off the storm with his jokes about the spelling. Best of all, he had spoken positively about Abby's going away to school.

She knew that if Aunt Ellen were too unhappy because of the rain and wind, and the big trees, Uncle John wouldn't want to stay. However, if Jack liked living here, then Aunt Ellen would be happy. It was plain as an owl's eyes that the one to work on was Jack.

All day long while she was working—cleaning, or bringing bark, or plucking the chickens ready for Mother to dress—she tried to think of ways to please Jack.

She might suggest that Henry take him soon on a canoe trip to the harbor. Then there was the hunting trip near home, and perhaps Jack could set some traps. She didn't like that idea so well, traps were cruel. Of course, a cougar was cruel too, and ought to be caught. Problems like that were hard to settle; Uncle John might have some solution.

At noon Mother put leftovers on the table. "Let's get these things cleaned up," she said. "There's a smidgen

of this and a dab of that; I want to get things cleaned up so there'll be more room on the shelves. We'll start fresh tomorrow."

Near the end of the morning Abby found time for a quick run up the road on Kloshe. She reported that there were no trees down for a mile beyond Browning's. "That is, on the road; there are some down back in the woods."

Mother told Clara she could play out in the yard if she bundled up and stayed in the sunshine. "You can listen for Father."

About the middle of the afternoon she came running in shouting, "Mother! I heard wagon wheels and people talking!"

They all followed Clara to the yard, ready to join in the welcome. Henry galloped up on Skookum, then the wagon rolled in with Father and Jack. One look at Father's face told Abby that everything had gone well on the trip.

For once, Jack talked fast and loud. He explained to his mother that it was a good thing he had gone along to help. "Uncle Will sure needed me. Coming back, near Hagdon's, there were trees down. We cut them and rolled them off the road. Then just after we crossed the Skook-umchuck Ferry there were a lot of trees across the road. The stage was going to start from Olympia about an hour after we did; I guess they were pretty glad we cleared the road. They couldn't make the regular trip yesterday because of the storm."

"Where were you yesterday?" his mother asked.

"I wandered around Olympia. I talked to some boys and men down on the waterfront and went into some of the stores. A town like that wouldn't be bad to live in. And do you know—I like to saw wood! Uncle Will bought a new crosscut, and with me on one end of it, we cleared the trees off in double-quick time."

Abby pretended not to hear him. She didn't need to brag about him; he was doing enough of it himself. It looked as if he could keep himself happy. She stood near the wagon and Father gave her parcels to carry in. One large one, he said, was for her Christmas; she could shake it but not open it. "That is to teach you patience."

Mother was peering over the side of the wagon bed. "My roses?" she asked.

"Here they are. I'll have to let you see your Christmas present now, so you can get it planted—a laburnum, a honeysuckle, and a lilac. One of these roses is something special, they said. I think it's called 'Hudson's Bay.' "

Mother held the bushes in her arms as carefully as if she were holding a baby. "Mrs. Browning has one she calls that. She grew it from a slip she got at the Jackson courthouse. It's pink, and single. I've wanted one since I first saw it."

Father lifted a sack that seemed to be heavy and slid it down the endgate to Jack. Water dripped through the cloth.

"What on earth is that, Will?" Aunt Ellen asked.

Mother looked. "I know; it's clams. He always brings some when he goes to the Sound."

Jack dragged the sack toward the house. "Father!" he called to Uncle John. "Wait till we get these turned into chowder. You'll be surprised and say that's about the best stuff you ever ate. I had some for supper last night."

Uncle John laughed. "You forget that your parents came from New England and that I lived in Boston for five years. You help me shuck these. Then while we do the chores, your mother can make us some chowder. She used to be a master hand at it and I don't believe she has forgotten."

"I'll cut up some salt pork and get it frying in the iron kettle; then some potatoes. . . ." Aunt Ellen hurried into the house.

"You men hustle with the chores," Mother said. "We can have an early supper and hear about the trip."

Everybody went to work and in no time they were at the table. The fire was extra bright and matched the gay spirits and the delicious smell of the chowder, Abby thought.

Aunt Ellen dished big bowls of the chowder while Mother and Abby put other things on.

"Chowder and brown bread and crullers—that's your supper tonight. There won't be so many dishes to wash, and we can get to bed early. We'll need an early start tomorrow."

"If I get hungry in the night, I know what I'll do," Father told her. "I saw all those things in the North Room ready for your party tomorrow. But this chowder hits the spot, all right."

"Yes, it's very good, Ellen," Uncle John said. "But nothing can beat that salmon that Henry cooked Sunday."

Before Abby thought, she said, "Isn't it nice living where there are so many fish, Jack?"

"You certainly are a booster, Abby," Father said. "Too bad old Doc White didn't get you to help sell his lots down at Pacific City. Right now, all the talk in Olympia is about the railroad. Every little town on the Sound thinks it should be the western terminal of the Northern Pacific. Olympia says it should be, since it is the capital of the Territory."

"I agree," Mother said. "When the railroad goes

through from Kalama next year, it should go right up to Olympia. And if they ever get through fighting over routes and quit losing money, the railroad from the East could come to Olympia. Think of the things we could buy!"

"It won't take me long to go to school if I can go from Saundersville to Olympia on the train," Abby said.

"Don't you ever think about anything but school?" Jack asked.

Abby didn't answer; she realized that she had broken her resolution about school twice already.

Henry moved over by the fireplace so he could do some whittling. Jack took a stool and sat by him. Henry was showing him how to make a trap.

Abby hurried to clear the table for she had promised Mother to polish the knives and forks for tomorrow. She gathered them up, washed them, and put them on the table with the brick dust. She knew she could scour and listen—and maybe talk—at the same time.

As usual, Jack was asking about ways to make money. Henry said there was good money cutting timbers for the California mines. "They're shipping them all the time from Whidbey Island, a man in Olympia told me. A little logging, with some money from trapping, ought to make all the money you need, Jack."

"I need all the money I can get," Jack replied. "It's the most important thing because it gets you everything else."

"Stories are more important," Abby said. "You can lose your money but you can't lose things you've learned. Tell us a story, Henry, please."

Henry drew a sharp stone along the seasoned branch of yew he was shaping into an ax handle. "All right, Abby, you've been working hard this week; I think you should have what you want."

Mother smiled at Aunt Ellen and they worked quietly so they could listen. Father took Clara on his lap. Uncle John settled back in his favorite chair.

"My mother was an Indian, you know," Henry began, "and she said this was a favorite story of her tribe. There was once an old miser who was always wanting more *hiaqua*."

"What is that?" Jack interrupted.

"They were shells the Indians used for money," Abby told him.

Henry went on. "Moos-moos, the elk, told Miser that up on The Mountain there were strings of *hiaqua* buried. He told him where to go to dig. Miser took some supplies of dried meat and camas cakes and slipped away so he wouldn't have to tell anyone where he was going. He climbed and climbed. At last, beyond where the trees grew, he came to three large stones. One looked like camas, one like a salmon, and one like an elk. He knew this was where he should dig.

"The first time Miser hit the ground an otter came out of a black pool that had suddenly appeared. Miser stopped digging, and the otter hit him with his tail. So

122

Miser dug again. At each stroke of his pick, an otter came out of the pool until there were thirteen sitting in a circle around him. And every time Miser stopped digging, an otter struck him.

"At last he found a string of *hiaqua*. He dug until he had twenty strings. As he lifted them into his bag, a storm began, a terrible storm, with wind and thunder. It swept over the bare top of The Mountain. The otter disappeared into the black pool, and the pool, too, disappeared. Miser picked up his bag and started down the slope, stumbling under his burden. He heard someone shouting after him, '*Hiaqua! Hiaqua!*'

"Miser tried to hurry, but the storm beat around him. He tried to lighten his burden and threw away one string of shells. The storm seemed to stop a little. He went on down, but the storm became worse. Now he was in the forest and the trees were crashing around. He could hear voices in the distance, '*Hiaqua! Hiaqua!*'

"He threw away the strings one by one, and each time the storm grew less. At last all the strings were gone, and the storm seemed to be over. Miser lay down to rest and went to sleep.

"When he woke, everything was changed. The trees were larger, the bushes thicker. He went on down The Mountain and at last came to a little cabin that looked like his, but the wood was crumbling; it was falling to pieces. A woman came to the door and Miser saw that it was his klootchman, only she looked very old. She told him that he had been gone thirty winters.

123

"Miser had no strings of *hiaqua* left, but he was satisfied. He made a garden and hunted and fished. He didn't care about *hiaqua* any more but he was happy."

"That was a good story, Henry," Jack said. "I suppose you told it because you thought I was worrying too much about money?"

Henry smoothed the ax handle carefully before he answered. "Well, young folks get the idea sometimes that money will buy everything. There's some things you can't get with money."

Uncle John spoke quietly. "I heard a man say once that the things you can't count are the things that count most."

Jack didn't argue, but Abby was sure that he still felt that money was very important. She couldn't blame him, for she knew that he wanted money so he could make things better for Aunt Ellen and Uncle John, not for himself.

Father came downstairs after putting Clara to bed, and sat down figuring in his little notebook. "Abby, I'll have about twenty dollars for you that I got when I sold your stock in Olympia. I'll get the exact account in a few days and tell you."

Abby ran and hugged him. "Father! Just think how much I'll be able to buy when I go away to school." Botheration! she thought. That resolution about school isn't broken; it's smashed. She looked at Jack and knew that he was unhappy because he didn't have any money. She planned quickly. "Father, couldn't Uncle John and

124

I help you all you need for a week or so, and let Henry and Jack go out hunting?"

Her father looked at her with the little grin he had when he knew she was scheming. "We-ell, maybe. Next week I think we are going to butcher, and I'll need all hands. After that, we'll see. But don't get too good, Abby, I like you better natural, not an angel."

"She'd better get to bed now," Mother said. "Tomorrow is the day of the quilting, and I'll need everybody, early."

"All hands saddled and in the corral at daybreak!" Henry called. He and Jack went out laughing.

Before Abby got into bed she shook the package that Father had said was her Christmas present. It certainly felt like goods for a dress. She remembered Mr. Washington's offer to sew for her. She put the package in the corner of the room where she could see it first thing when she opened her eyes.

CHAPTER Seven

Friday's weather seemed made to order for a party. Everyone felt a responsibility and was stirring around by the time Father had the kettle boiling in the fireplace.

Abby was hustling things to the table when her uncle came in whistling. That reminded her of something.

"Uncle John, you haven't played your violin for me yet. I hope we have time for it soon. Do you know, the very first money that I earn teaching is going to be spent for an organ. I want a melodeon like that one Mrs. Judson has; it was brought around the Horn and it cost a hundred dollars. Took a year to bring it. Maybe they are cheaper now."

That made Mother cross. "Abby, was there ever such a girl to plan ahead? Get your mind on what your work is for today. As soon as we have finished breakfast, I want you to help Father take the bed down in our room and put the bedding away. Then we'll have a place for the women to be comfortable around the quilting frame."

Soon everything was ready. Mother and Aunt Ellen had put the new quilt into the frames on Wednesday. It seemed to Abby there was always a quilt in the frames. When Mother was not working on it, she pulled it up to the ceiling, out of the way.

Father had made this arrangement with ropes and a pulley. He said he got the idea from President Jefferson, who pulled his bed to the ceiling during the day. Abby was sure it was one of Father's jokes, a President wouldn't do that. Today, with the bed out of the room, there was a place for the women to sit around the frames.

Mrs. Davis and Mrs. Mills came first. They said the days were so short that they wanted to use all the daylight there was. Then Mrs. Browning came with Mary Adeline Borst, who was visiting her for a few days. Abby was glad to see her, for Mary Adeline's tongue went as fast as her fingers, and the party was sure to be gay. Nettie Browning came a little later with Mrs. Clinger. Soon stools were pulled up and the women were hard at work stitching.

"It's a pretty pattern, Mrs. Watson; what did you say you called it?" Mrs. Davis asked.

"One of my neighbors in Kansas brought it from her home in Pennsylvania," Aunt Ellen answered. "She said it was a Dutch pattern. They called it 'Star and Crescent' at first, but later someone named it 'Hearts and Gizzards.'"

The women laughed and agreed that they liked "Star and Crescent" better.

"I pieced it last winter. We were snowed in for weeks with a Kansas blizzard. I was glad that just before the storm my mother and some friends in Vermont had sent me a big package of pretty pieces and some thread and needles. I'll cut the pattern off for anyone who wants it," Aunt Ellen finished.

"I'd admire to have it," little Mrs. Mills said. "Maybe sometime I can afford to get all new material, two plain colors and a print. That would make me a best quilt. This brown sprigged with rosebuds is mighty pretty."

"Come spring, I'll have a 'Log Cabin' ready to quilt," Mrs. Davis said. "I never get tired of that pattern. This time I'm setting it together in a new way they call 'Straight Furrow'; it was in our *Agriculturist*. Underneath they had this quotation, almost like poetry. I like it extremely well, and learned it. 'Let me not look behind, but to the hilltop ahead. May the next furrow be straighter than the last.'"

Everyone was quiet for a minute. Abby knew she would remember the quotation—school was her hilltop. Then Mary Adeline spoke up in her quick way.

"Come on, let's get busy. We have done only one roll and we must get two more rolls finished before we eat. He that works not, neither shall he eat."

They laughed, as usual, at Mary Adeline, but they started working again.

Abby scurried into the kitchen, although she hated to miss the talk. She wanted to be sure that everything was cooking, for Mother was counting on her.

Nettie Browning went with her. She said she had come to help Abby, but Abby wondered whether she would have been so anxious to help if Jack hadn't been visiting. She was sure of it when Nettie looked around and out the window.

"Where are the men—and your cousin?" she asked.

Abby busied herself with the cooking before she answered. She was only now realizing how nosy Nettie was. It made her mad. "The men? Uncle John said he was going to take a ride to the store and the mill; he didn't think he was needed for what he calls Aunt Ellen's 'coming-out party.' And the others are doing their work, I suppose. Why?" Abby had found out that it put people in a tizzy if you asked them "Why?"

"Why?" Nettie was flustered. "I—don't know." She giggled. "I thought maybe you were keeping Jack locked up, he never goes to see anyone except with you. But, after all, he's your cousin, so——"

"He's not——" Abby stopped. Maybe she oughtn't to say that Jack was adopted.

"Not what?" Now Nettie was curious.

"Not happy out here. I think they'll go back in the spring." Abby saw her scheme had worked when Nettie replied.

"Well, I don't blame them. There must be more interesting things back East."

Abby pretended not to hear. She liked to tell Nettie things but she simply was not going to talk about the Watsons and why she wanted them to stay out in Washington Territory. She hurried back and forth, getting the table set and bringing things from the North Room. She dished the dinner, then called the quilters and got them seated to eat.

Mother and Aunt Ellen passed the ham and pickles and other things that were on the table; Abby flew around getting the hot dishes, especially pieces of chicken pie with the brown gravy bubbling over the crust. She poured coffee, although first everyone tried the tea that Aunt Ellen had brought from San Francisco, a Chinese tea with flowers in it.

They agreed with Mary Adeline, who said she liked coffee best, even the kind they made from beans or bran and molasses. "I suppose that isn't really coffee," she said, "but I don't know what else to call it, and it takes the place of coffee."

The women said they were eating so much that it would be hard to work. Abby knew they meant it, although they would have said it to be polite. She was proud that Mother was considered one of the best cooks in the country. She would try to remember to tell Jack that Aunt Ellen's cooking had been praised very highly.

After the quilting had been resumed, Father peeked in the door like he was scared and asked whether it was safe for a hungry man to come in and beg for some scraps. The women laughed—people always laughed at the things Father said. Abby told him to bring the men in, that she and Nettie had washed the dishes and set the table; now she'd hunt a few scraps to put on.

Abby maneuvered to put Nettie on the bench by Uncle John so she wouldn't sit next to Jack. Then she saw her mistake, for Nettie could smirk across the table at him and roll her eyes.

"How do you like the Wild West, Mr. Watson?" she asked Uncle John.

130

"I like it fine," he answered. "The food out here is wonderful."

"He was glad to get away from the grasshoppers back in Kansas," Henry said. "And what do you think? They waste the 'hoppers back there; Watson tells me they never used them. Now even Indians know better than that; they hunt them."

"Hunt them?" Jack asked. "You don't really mean— hunt?"

"Oh, yes. The Indians dig a big hole, not very deep, and spread round it in a big circle, out on the prairie. They close in, driving the 'hoppers before them into the hole, and then kill them."

"What did they want them for?"

Abby sighed. She knew the story and was sorry he'd asked.

Henry grinned at Abby. "Well, first they baked the 'hoppers on stones they had heated, or dried them out in the sun. Then they pounded them to a powder, the way they pounded their corn on a big flat rock. They mixed them with service berries that they'd mashed to a jam, put in a little camas flour, made the mixture into little flat cakes, dried them in the sun—there's your fruitcake!"

Jack made a face. "Well, we never had to eat anything like that in Kansas," Jack said.

"No, but remember we got pretty hungry sometimes," his father reminded him. "I'm sure that during the war we would have welcomed those cakes. Our hardtack was likely to have little live ' 'hoppers' in it."

131

"Yes, I've seen many times on the trail when that fruitcake tasted good," Henry insisted.

"You mean—you have eaten it?" Jack sounded unconvinced.

"Sure. You get stuck in the desert without food and you're not too pernickety."

Abby was glad to have Father change the subject by talking about things in Vermont. If Henry told too many queer stories about food, Jack would have one more reason for not wanting to stay in the Territory.

Nettie asked Jack if he liked parties, and did he dance.

Abby wanted to giggle at Jack's short answer.

"Not much."

Abby felt a little sorry for Nettie when Jack wouldn't talk to her. After all, Nettie was one of her best friends, and Mother would say that she must always be nice to a guest. So after the men went out and the two girls were clearing up and washing the dishes, Abby told Nettie all she knew about the Watsons' trip West. She explained that she thought Uncle John was especially nice because he was helping her with some school lessons.

"You're queer," Nettie said. "Why do you want to keep on going to school?"

"You're queer if you don't want to go!" Abby answered.

Before it was dark, the quilt was finished except for the edge that Mother and Aunt Ellen would do later. Mother brought everyone to the table for pie and cake and coffee. They asked Aunt Ellen about her trip, and Mary Adeline wanted to know what the latest styles were in San Francisco.

"I didn't have much time in San Francisco," Aunt Ellen said. "The boat for Portland left the day after our train came in. Maybe you would like to see a dress I brought with me. When I wrote my mother that we were coming West, she said she would give me a dress that would be nice for afternoon tea. She sent to Boston for the material and had it made from a pattern in *Godey's*. I haven't shown it to Julia yet. You can see my mother doesn't have much idea what the West is like."

She went to the trunk in the corner of the bedroom and brought out a dress that made them all gasp.

"It's beautiful!" Mary Adeline said. "Look at those knife-plaited ruffles on the circular skirt! There are five of them; that flowered silk is lovely with the pongee."

"I like the way the polonaise loops over on the side," Mrs. Browning said. "Do you know how much goods is in it?"

"My mother said there were twenty yards of the pongee and five of the flowered silk," Aunt Ellen answered. "I don't know how much China silk there is in the skirt lining. I'm going to rip it up and make a dress each for Julia and me, and use the flowered for a dress for Abby. Even if we don't stay out West, I don't expect to live where I would have use for such a dress."

"Such a lot of work on it." Mrs. Mills ran her hand over the soft silk. "It's a pity to rip it up."

"But imagine how those ruffles and loops would get caught every time she went to put wood on the fireplace!" Mary Adeline said. "May I come over someday and try it on before you rip it up? And you come to see me and I'll show you the dress I wore when I led the Grand March at the Governor's Ball in Olympia—years ago, when I was young and gay. But I still like pretty clothes."

"Speaking of Olympia reminds me." Mrs. Browning turned to Mother. "Nettie and I are going there in about a month to visit my aunt. Could Abby go with us? She and Nettie would have a good time together, and I know my aunt would like to have her. Maybe you can spare her now that your sister is here."

"Let the child go," Mrs. Mills said. "Our girls don't have many treats."

Abby held her breath—and her tongue. Mother didn't like coaxing.

"It's kind of you to offer to take the trouble, Mrs. Browning," Mother told her. "We'll see."

Abby knew that meant she would ask Father, so as soon as the guests had gone she hustled about the work. That would please him and make him more likely to say yes.

She cleared up and washed the dishes while Mother and Aunt Ellen folded the quilt carefully and put the needles and thread away. When Father came in she put on her cape and hood and went out so he and Mother could talk alone. Jack loaded a wheelbarrow with some of the bark they had gathered and Abby picked up small

branches of fir that had blown down and added them to the fireplace fuel.

Father and Henry were putting up the bed, so she went in with the bedding and tried to help.

"A certain person seems to be work-brittle tonight, Julia. Did you say it was a month before Mrs. Browning is going to Olympia?" Father asked. "We can get a lot of work done before that if we plan it right. Nothing like holding hay in front of the donkey's nose!"

Abby pretended she didn't hear him. She might have known he'd catch on to her working extra hard. She was happy, anyway, for it meant he hadn't said she couldn't go.

Mother put on a cold supper, since they were all sure they weren't hungry. Still, Jack took several slices of ham and venison, Abby noticed. While they were eating she went to the cupboard drawer and took out a paper.

"Listen, Father, please. This is from the Washington *Standard*. It is advice to a girl. Of course, it says that a girl shouldn't be vain, and that it is wicked to waste time. Everybody says that. This is the main thing: 'If you can, cultivate to perfection some art by which you can gain an independent livelihood. Do it quietly, if you will, but do it. There is no telling when or under what circumstances you may need it.' And the *Standard* had reprinted it from the *Demorest Magazine*. So you see it must be important, and it shows that I should learn to teach."

" 'Do it quietly, if you will . . .' " Father read, and laughed.

"Watch out, Will," Uncle John said. "Sounds to me as if you had a politician in your family! Some people back East say that women ought to vote. Next thing you know, they'll be running for office."

Aunt Ellen went to the fireplace and began stirring a kettle of grits, hard, as if she were in earnest. "Well, I guess women could do as good a job of running the country as the men have. One thing, I read that women say if they could vote they'd try not to have any war; that there's no sense in it. I agree."

Father smoothed Abby's hair as she sat beside him with the paper. "Mother tells me that Mrs. Browning has invited you to go to Olympia with her. I think we can manage it if——"

Abby hugged him so hard he said he couldn't breathe.

"Father! You'll see! I'll just help and help with the work." She remembered that the important thing was for Jack to be happy, so she added, "Maybe, before I go, Henry and Jack could have that hunting trip?"

"Don't forget that I told you last night I'd have to see how the work went next week. Perhaps they can."

Abby went to bed with her mind buzzing with plans. She wanted to go to the stores in Olympia and maybe she would have time to visit a school and find out how she could enroll in one, even though Nettie wouldn't care for that. And in the Olympia paper there had been a notice about a play that was coming to town. She ought to see that, even if she had to spend some of the money she was saving. Miss Peebles had told them lots about plays; she even read them some Shakespeare. She started with *Macbeth*, and the boys liked that so well they were willing to listen to more. Miss Peebles read poetry so beautifully that Abby almost cried. She would learn to read it that way before she taught school. A person was willing to learn arithmetic, or even physiology, from a teacher who could read interesting things. Abby had learned special bits by heart and went to sleep saying, " 'Out, damned spot!' " and " 'Beggars, that come unto my father's door . . .' " Katherine was about her favorite, she guessed. Miss Peebles had let her read it several times. That was another thing she would buy with her schoolteaching money—Shakespeare.

CHAPTER **Eight**

A hard frost brought the kind of weather Father wanted for the butchering at exactly the time he planned it.

"The moon is in the first quarter, as it should be," Henry told them.

"Well, I'm glad to know that. Let's get to work," Father said. He always poked fun at Henry for watching the phases of the moon to decide when to plant vegetables, or to go fishing, or to butcher; but Abby noticed that he listened to Henry.

Mr. Mills promised to send one of his boys to help with the butchering. Abby hurried through her work, and when she saw the boy going to the barn she rushed out and saddled Kloshe. She would ride for an hour or so, then she'd be sure that everything was over before she came back. She knew that butchering had to be done, but she simply couldn't stay and listen to the squealing. Mother always looked as if she would like to leave, too.

Abby slipped away before Mother could ask her to take Clara. Even Mother didn't know where she went on these solitary rides. She knew that Abby liked to ride up by the Claquato church, where she looked out from the Bluff over the river, but she didn't know about Abby's "hide-out," as she called it. She had found a huge cedar stump one day not far behind the Davises' old log house. It was completely hidden from the road, but Kloshe had been over it with her so many times that he would push through the brush as soon as she headed him that way. First, over the brow of the hill. If anyone saw her going, he would think she were riding down to the Flats. Abby was afraid that if she rode over it too often, a path would be worn. So she left her pony in a different place in the brush each time and pushed her way through the hazelnut and salal bushes, over fallen trees and by big fir stumps. She thought Mr. Davis must have logged this over for the big trees when he homesteaded there.

Her cedar stump was hollow, and she had sneaked some shingles from home, a few at a time, and made a little roof. It was like a tiny house—as a matter of fact, she knew that pioneers had lived in cedar stumps while they were building their cabins.

When she knew she would have an hour or more free, she brought some bread and butter with her, but she always brought a book. Today she began reading *Ivanhoe* for the fourth time. Once she had been so interested that she read until almost dark and Mother had scolded about her riding so far away. She didn't want to say that she had been only a mile and a half away. If her hide-out was discovered, it wouldn't be any good to her. She wanted to be alone and read or dream comfortably resting on the big pile of dry moss. One day when she had been visiting Mr. Lum he gave her an hourglass that he had brought from the East. Now she carried it with her and could watch to see how time was going.

Today, when the last bit of sand had gone through she got up, reluctantly. She knew that there was work at home, and there was no use getting in trouble about being late.

When she reached the yard, she saw the men scalding the pigs, so her part would come soon. She put Kloshe into the pasture and went to work getting small wood and bark. She carried the fuel to the big iron kettle that hung in the side yard on a bar between two supports. Abby wanted to do most of the soapmaking; it wasn't hard, and she liked to hear folks brag about what good soap she could make.

First, though, the kettle would be needed to render the lard. During the afternoon Mother cut up the best of the leaf lard into tiny pieces and put it into the kettle with a little bit of water. Abby stirred with a long wooden paddle, and kept just enough fire going so the grease bubbled gently out. Mother scooped this out and strained it into big stone jars. There were rich brown cracklings left. Aunt Ellen cooked some spoon bread in the Dutch oven and that, with the cracklings and molasses, was what Abby called a perfect supper dish.

Henry put a wooden cover he had made over the kettle to keep it clean, and the next morning Abby tried out what Mother called her second-best lard. That was from other butchering fat.

After the lard was in the jars, all the rest of the fat, with bits of grease that Mother had been saving, was put in the kettle and Abby rendered that and strained it for her soap.

Jack came out to watch her and she explained how she got the lye.

"Father made this hopper out of split cedar shakes. You see, it's square, and wider at the top, so it tapers to this small opening at the bottom, where we put clean

straw. Father laid crushed limestone on the straw; that makes the strainer. For a few days in the summer we burned only hardwood in the fireplace, then gathered the ashes and filled the hopper. When it was heaping full, I set it over a stone jar, poured boiling water through— and there is the lye for my soap! I had to have it all ready before this week, of course."

"You make pretty good soap, if that's what I've been using," Jack said.

"Good for a girl to make, I suppose you mean?" Abby grinned, and stuck her tongue out at him.

"Oh, I guess girls are useful," Jack admitted. "Anyway, you are the best girl I ever saw."

He walked quickly away before she could answer, but his words stayed in her mind while she was working. Jack was funny; he would say things to her when they were alone that were nice—almost like poetry. Then he usually didn't seem even to see her when the grownups were around. Boys were queer.

Each had his own work to do this busy week and was hustling around in the clear frosty air. Mother planned and cooked most of the meals, and saw to it that the house was clean. Jack and his father did a good many of the chores, and Aunt Ellen and Uncle John said they wanted to take over the sausage and head cheese.

Henry never would let anyone do the hams and bacon. First, he smoked wooden kegs and put the meat in to cure in a sort of brine. Nobody knew his receipt; all he would say was that it was a French-Canuck way that he had learned from a Hudson's Bay man. He had built a special little smoke house. Abby was never sure just what wood he used, but she thought it was alder mixed with scrub oak. Henry wouldn't admit it, but she knew he was very proud when people praised his meat.

Abby managed to get into all the activities, but the soap was her real specialty. First she made soft soap that was best for washing dishes. The next day three or four gallons of the soft soap was put back in the kettle with a little more lye. As it boiled, Abby stirred in salt until it got white and curdly-looking. Then she stirred and boiled until a spoonful would harden quickly when she took it out. When the fire went out and the soap was getting cool, Father poured it into wooden trays he had constructed with tight sides. Before it hardened Abby cut it into cakes that were easy to take out.

Mother had sent for some sassafras essence and alcohol when the men went to Olympia. She brought out a copper kettle and helped with a new receipt for toilet soap. They put in some of the best of the soft soap and mixed the alcohol with it, letting it get hot gradually. When it was dissolved, Abby stirred the sassafras in and mixed it, then poured it into pans. To her great delight, it turned out transparent and very sweet-smelling. Mother said she might wrap up two cakes to give Nettie at Christmas time.

Sometimes, when Abby stood pushing the long paddle back and forth in the kettle, and looking up at the tall fir trees waving their branches with cones in the sunlight, or watching the chipmunks dash around gathering hazelnuts for their winter "North Room," she thought it would be more fun to stay home than to go away to school.

But that was laziness, for a person couldn't learn to be a teacher by making soap and gawking at the trees; and to be a teacher was what she wanted more than anything else.

Molding candles was another job Abby liked and always asked to do. Two years before, Father had given Mother a big oil lamp for Christmas. They used it on the table, where it cast a fine yellow circle. Abby pretended that it was a ring of gold that held them all together.

However, they needed lots of candles for the bedrooms and the lanterns. Abby said that Jack could help her and in two or three evenings they could make enough.

In the spring Father had killed a sheep and cured the hide for a lining for his work jacket. Mother had rendered the tallow and saved it for candles. They had some beeswax and alum to mix so it wouldn't get too soft when it was warm. Abby was likely to brag that her candles stood up straight even in the summer.

The molds each held four candles, and they had six molds. By starting early and filling the molds once before supper, they made four dozen each evening.

Father had brought good new wicking. Abby showed Jack how to run a length through the mold and tie two knots to keep the tallow from running out. The other end they looped tightly over a stick. They took turns holding the molds and pouring the hot tallow in. The molds were set in a rack outdoors to cool; after the tallow was hard they cut the knot, dipped the molds quickly in hot water, and pulled the candles out by the loop on the stick.

One evening after supper Uncle John showed Abby a smooth cedar board he had brought in. "Look, I want to teach you something." He had some soft pieces of charcoal and began to draw with them. "You want to learn to play the organ, you said; we'll make a start. These are the keys I'm drawing on here. Get your slate, and I'll teach you a rhyme."

"That looks just like an organ!" Abby exclaimed when she hurried back. "What do I write?"

*"All the G and A keys are between the black threes,
And between the black twos are all the Ds.
On the right of the threes will be found Bs and Cs,
But at left of the threes are the Fs and the Es."*

Abby took her slate and sat back in the corner studying. She muttered the lines over and over; Henry said she sounded like an Indian medicine man.

"In a day or so, when you have that learned, I'll teach you what it means," Uncle John promised.

Jack grumbled because she wouldn't play checkers with him. "I never saw anyone so crazy about school. What good is that music going to do you?"

"Every day I'll open my school with prayer and two or three songs," Abby answered. "I want to learn lots of songs. Anyway, music makes me happier. Don't you want me to be happy?"

"Do you know this song, Abby?" Uncle John began to sing. "Oh my darling, oh my darling, oh my darling Clementine."

"That's fun! Please sing it until I learn it."

So he sang it again and again. Mother and Aunt Ellen joined Abby in singing, and she heard even Jack humming.

Then her uncle sang a new song that he said they learned at the Knights Templar meetings in Kansas. "Home, Sweet Home."

They all sang it three times, then sat looking at the fire. No one spoke. Abby didn't like that; she knew that if she sang it too often she wouldn't want to leave home. Probably it was making Jack homesick for Kansas. She was trying to think of something lively to say to change the subject, when Uncle John spoke.

"Will, I rode down to Davis's mill today." His voice was solemn, the way people talk when they have something special to tell.

Father chuckled. "Did you watch them saw? Sometimes I think it would be fun to have a job there. There's no hurry; you can sit on one end of a log and eat your lunch before you get to the muley saw!"

"I felt the same way," Uncle John answered, "so I got a job there."

"You did what, Father?" Jack sounded as if he thought his father couldn't work.

Abby was afraid her uncle's feelings were hurt, so she tried to reassure him. "I'm sure they would be glad to have you, Uncle John, but what would I do without your help?" She hoped that might teach Jack some manners.

Uncle John smiled. "This isn't much of a job, Abby. We'll have lots of time together. You see, Will, they need someone to keep track of their buying and selling, and to write letters, now that they have more business with their flour and lumber. I told them that I had kept books, and that I would be glad to help and trade my work for lumber, or flour. Might need the lumber for a house."

"Oh!" Jack and Abby spoke together, but the two "Ohs" didn't seem to have the same meaning.

"Whose house?" Jack almost growled.

"Ours, in case we decide to stay," His father used the tone that always silenced Jack. "Your uncle Will can use it if we don't stay out West."

Jack looked at his mother. She didn't speak for a minute, then said, "It's for you to decide, John."

Abby jumped up before Jack could say anything. If she could get him to eating, he wouldn't talk, and maybe after a while he would feel better.

"Mother," she said, "I forgot to tell you, Mrs. Browning sent you some crullers today when I was at the store. Let's have them with some hot cider. Jack, you help me, please."

She poured cider into a kettle, and put in three cinnamon sticks and a few cloves. "Swing that over the fire, Jack, while I get the crullers and some cups."

Father winked at her, but she pretended not to notice. He always caught on to her schemes. But he began to tell a story, so she knew he was helping her to change the subject.

"That seems like a good idea, John, you'll be a great help to them. Henry, I heard an idea in Olympia that I wish you would try if you and Jack go to the harbor next week. It's a good way to keep fish if you want to carry them a few days."

"Let's hear it."

"As soon as you take them off the hook, open their mouths and put a little brandy down their throats. Then soak breadcrumbs in brandy and fill their mouths. They stay alive, you see, but they go to sleep. Pack them in straw. When you get home, turn them loose in water. They'll wake up and there you have fresh fish to eat."

Henry laughed. "Maybe that would work, but I think I'll take a few pounds of salt along. Cheaper, and I'm used to that way of keeping fish. I figured we'd take a canoe, Jack, and go down the Chehalis to the Harbor. It's easy going down, and not too much work coming back. We have to portage around some falls, but just short pieces."

Jack nodded, but didn't answer. He's still sulking, Abby thought. My goodness, it's a lot of trouble to keep him happy. Maybe it isn't worth it. If Uncle John would stay, Jack could leave for all of me. Still, she thought, Jack is fun sometimes. He had been happier lately when they were working at the candles and all.

149

Father got up and went toward the stairs. "You know, Julia, this singing has made me feel that this is like Christmas. What do you say if we pretend that it's Abby's Christmas, anyway?"

Mother smiled and nodded. "She could use it on the trip with Mrs. Browning, when she goes to Olympia."

Abby held her breath. Was he going to get that package he had brought? She shook it every night, but she hadn't peeked inside. Sure enough, he carried it down and put it into her lap.

"Remember, this is what Mother and I are giving you for your Christmas—just a little early."

She shook it and felt it. "Well, look at it," Jack said.

She untied the string and slowly pulled the paper away. There were yards and yards of blue, thin wool; exactly the color of forget-me-nots, exactly the color she wanted for a dress.

"Oh, Mother, Father!" She gave her mother a kiss and threw her arms around her father. "How did you know the color to get?"

"Hey, you're choking me!" he said. But he let her put her head on his shoulder. She was sure that nobody noticed that way that she was wiping her eyes.

Father patted her. "Thought maybe your mother and Ellen could make it up for you to wear in Olympia. Can't have the folks there saying that we don't know what style is here in Claquato."

She sat up. "Can you, Mother? I know the way I want it made—flounces, and full. Please make it a little large for me, and with a big hem, so I can still wear it when I go to teaching. For a best dress, of course."

"Always talking about that teaching," Jack grumbled, but he smiled at her. Maybe he wasn't as cross as he talked.

She wrapped her material carefully and went to the stairs. "Guess I'd better go to bed; then I can get up early to work." She waited a minute. "Do you think you'll have time to sew my dress, Mother?"

"With Aunt Ellen here I think we can. Mrs. Browning is very kind to help with cutting things; she has that dressmaker's chart at the store. Probably I could do some of the long seams on Mrs. Washington's machine," Mother replied. "We'll see. You go to bed and stop worrying."

"Well, I was thinking that if you don't have time, I could ask Mr. Washington to sew it. Perhaps I didn't tell you, but that time I was down there, he said that he'd like to make me a dress sometime."

Abby went on up the stairs. She tiptoed into the room so she wouldn't wake Clara. First, she put the bundle of goods under her pillow, but she was afraid it would get wrinkled there. She wanted it close to her, so she pulled the stool close by the bed and put the goods on that. She went to sleep holding to one corner. This would be the prettiest dress she had ever had.

In the morning Abby looked at the blue goods all the time she was dressing. Then she put it on a high shelf that Clara couldn't reach. It would be like that child to take it for a bed for her dolls, she thought.

151

CHAPTER **Nine**

At breakfast Aunt Ellen asked Henry what clothes Jack should have ready for the harbor trip.

Henry looked surprised. "Why, what he has on, Mrs. Watson. Might take an extra pair of socks; maybe another shirt. We'll probably get wet; dry clothes would be handy."

Aunt Ellen was disturbed. "You won't have to stay out in the wet, will you?" she asked.

"Jack can take an old mackinaw of mine," Father said. "He won't get too wet."

"If we do, we'll just build a fire and dry out," Henry said impatiently, and went out.

"Please don't fuss about me, Mother," Jack said. "I can do what other men do."

On Saturday Jack talked to Abby about taking the bear cub and cougar into the woods. "I fixed the pen so Tilly never gets out any more; don't think that duck would make good eating," he said teasingly. "But that other pen won't hold those other animals much longer. They ought to be in the woods and used to getting their own food before winter comes."

Abby knew he was right, although it made her very sad. She hadn't told anyone that little cougar had torn

152

her sleeve and scratched her arm a few days before when she was slow getting his feed in. And the fawn was teasing the bear cub so he often was cross and growled at her.

"All right," she said, "we'll go early this afternoon."

Father had heard them talking and said that he would take Jack in the wagon with the pets. "And you stay home, Abby," he ordered. "Like as not right at the last minute you'd want to bring them back."

"I'll go with you," Henry said. "I brought them in, so I feel responsible. I never thought Abby would want to keep them when they were so big."

Abby wiped her eyes. "They are like friends. They don't seem like animals. Please, Father, take them back into the woods where they can find other deer and bears. The cougar can look out for himself, I think."

"I want you to go to the store, Abby," Mother said. "Get your riding clothes on. You can take Kloshe and go for a ride, first."

Abby went down to Saunders' Flats. She knew that Father would go the other way. Down there was a level stretch and she let the pony gallop; the frosty weather had made him frisky, and he hadn't had enough exercise. As she came back the stage was driving down to the ferry, and she decided to go to watch it cross. Funny, all the times she had seen that stage and she never had a ride on it. Well, she would be going on it in about two weeks. That thought cheered her, so she rode back to the store and had a visit with Nettie, discussing what they would wear in Olympia and what they would do.

"I wish there would be a circus in town," Nettie said, "but I guess they come only in the summer."

"I hope there is a play we can see," Abby told her.

By the time Abby got home, she saw that Father was out doing the chores. Jack had a wheelbarrow of wood at the door. She made up her mind she wouldn't go near the pets' pen that night.

"Will you feed the chickens and do my other chores, Jack?" she asked. "After I set the table I'm going to read; I'm tired."

He gave a grunt, but didn't say that he wouldn't. She changed her clothes, set the table, and then took *Little Women* and sat by the fire. That was such a wonderful book for any mood; it made her feel better.

Sunday was a stormy day, so Father hitched up the wagon and took the family to church. When they got home, they found Henry had dinner ready, as usual. This time it was pork roast with browned potatoes, steamed cabbage, and some wheat hominy they had made the week before. For dessert they had Indian pudding that Aunt Ellen had set to bake early that morning.

"This is extra good," Mother said. "I should have watched to see how you made it."

"The cornmeal they grind at Davis's mill is partly responsible," Aunt Ellen replied, "but this is a very good recipe. It's the one they use at Wright Tavern, in Massachusetts; they've made Indian pudding this way since before the Revolution."

While they were eating the pudding she asked Henry what food they would need for the harbor trip. He had said that they were leaving the next morning.

Abby noticed that Henry had been extra nice to her aunt since the morning he had been angry at her. She guessed he was trying to make up for being cross. After all, everyone knew that Aunt Ellen found things in the Territory strange, and of course she thought that the sun came up especially to shine on Jack.

"Not a thing, thank you, ma'am," Henry answered. "I've flour and salt and a chunk of bacon in the grub box. That's all we need, we'll catch the rest. Oh, maybe you could pack up a little coffee and a few potatoes."

"You should have seen the lunch we brought on the train when we left Kansas, Abby," Jack said. "Mother had packed a basketful and at the last minute one neighbor brought in two roast chickens, and another had a chocolate cake for us."

Abby grinned. "And I can see you now, eating at least half."

After an early breakfast Monday morning they began loading the wagon. Father was taking them to the river. They loaded in the grub box, blankets, and tarp, and then put the canoe on top.

Aunt Ellen began to worry. She said she never had seen anyone travel in a canoe; it looked very small. Wouldn't it likely tip over?

"A canoe is a safe way to ride, Ellen," Father said. "Especially with someone who knows how to handle it

the way Henry does. I'd rather ride with him in this than to go in a big boat."

"We won't be gone many days, Mrs. Watson," Henry said. "I promise that we won't go out into the ocean."

"You girls can ride down to the river with us," Father said, so Abby and Clara hustled into their heavy capes and hoods and climbed up on the seat with him.

Watching them put the canoe into the river and load it was fun. There was lots of room; Abby thought they might as well have taken her with them. She'd heard Henry say that Decker, who had sold him the canoe, often carried 125 bushels of potatoes in it.

When Jack said good-by, Abby gave him a small roll to put in his pocket. "Here are two candles," she said. "You can't tell when or where you might need them. Henry has a whole bunch of China matches."

"I'm not planning to spend the evenings reading," Jack said gruffly, but he took them.

Father and the girls watched and waved until a turn of the river took the travelers out of sight; then drove home.

The table seemed empty that day, and Abby sat glumly and tried not to eat. She had lost her pets; she didn't get to go on trips. Any heroine she had read about would just play with her food and soon grow pale and thin. Abby was disgusted with herself because she liked the supper so well. Mother had fried sausage in a skillet and poured cream over it before she took it up. Aunt Ellen took spoon bread from the Dutch oven. There were parsnips fried in butter, and dried corn. Abby sighed and gave up. Might as well eat; from some things she had heard Mother say, there was going to be work that would take strength.

While she wiped the dishes for Aunt Ellen, Abby recited the organ rhyme several times. Uncle John heard her and brought out the "organ board" as he called it.

"Soon as you are through, Abby," he called, "come sit here by the fire and I'll give you a music lesson."

That was so exciting that before she knew it, bedtime came.

Mother had planned so much work that there was no time to mope over missing a nice trip.

"Your new dress will have to wait until next week," she told Abby. "Tomorrow we'll get at the North Room. Your father says he will want to store this year's vegetables and fruit soon and there's no telling what day Henry will want to put the meat away. Likely he'll bring salmon on this trip, and soon there will be kegs of salt fish to be stored."

Uncle John said that he would like to help clean the North Room. "Can't you and I do it, Abby?" he asked. "Do you remember the first night I was here you told me about the North Room, and how safe it made you feel?"

Abby nodded. Somehow his remembering that made a lump come into her throat.

"Well," he went on, "I feel a great affection for this room too. It begins to mean to me work, and gathered harvests, and family—and a happier future."

With her uncle talking like that, the work seemed nothing at all. They took out all last year's vegetables and cleaned the bins and scrubbed them. Mother mixed a whitewash with a little copperas in it and they painted the bins and the shelves with this.

Abby measured newspapers for the shelves and cut scallops so they hung over the edges. The bottles of fruit were arranged in rows, "like soldiers marching," Uncle John said.

"I'm glad you can't make the blue dress this week," she told her mother. "I can't quite make up my mind which style I want." Every day, when she had a few minutes, she looked at *Peterson's Magazine* and every day she decided on a different way to make it. She wanted it to last for several years and it was hard to find a style that was good for a girl of thirteen and also for a young lady of sixteen. Still, planning things was as much fun as doing them—almost.

Aunt Ellen found time to unpack her books and she gave Abby lessons in Wilson's *History*. Uncle John read Wells' *The Science of Common Things* with her every evening. After that, they worked on the keyboard and learned new songs. Three afternoons the work went along so smoothly—Aunt Ellen was a fast worker, like Mother —that Abby had a chance to take a ride on Kloshe. She went to her hide-out and worked, making the roof over the stump a little tighter and clearing out more space inside. It was large enough to lie down in, so she gathered cedar boughs one day when the sun had been shining on them and they were dry and made a bed. She was afraid to do any pounding for fear she would be heard; she put a piece of an old Indian mat that Mother had thrown away and covered the roof with that. It was woven of bark, and as it got wet, it shrunk and kept more of the rain out.

Altogether, the week had had so many pleasant adventures that she was surprised when Father said one morning at breakfast, "Well, if our hunters keep their word and stay only a week, they'll be home in a couple days."

"They will?" Abby asked. "Of course, this is Saturday. Let's do some spelling tonight, Uncle John. Monday evening I guess we'll be listening to stories of their trip and won't have time for lessons or songs."

"I hope they haven't had any bad trouble," Aunt Ellen sighed. "I'm not sure that Jack should have gone when he is so new to this country."

"Best way to get over being a tenderfoot is to go off with an old-timer like Henry," Father said. "Don't worry, Ellen, unless you don't want Jack to stay out here. I'll bet he'll come home with pitch in his hair."

Abby thought of what Father had said all the next day, and began counting the hours until they might come. She had started to wash the dinner dishes Monday when Jack walked in.

"Hello, anything here to eat?" he asked.

His mother threw her arms around him and everyone had questions.

"Where's Henry?" Father asked.

"Down at the river, watching our load. Wait till you see all we brought! I came up to ask you to take the wagon down. I'll go back to help, but I want a bite to eat first. Abby, wasn't there anything left from dinner? I smell something good!"

Mother brought a plate of food; Abby poured a cup of coffee, but Aunt Ellen had to ask whether he was all right. "Did you see any Indians? Did you have enough to eat?"

"Good trip." Jack nodded and crammed some pie down. "I must go with Uncle Will—tell you all about it later, Mother." He rushed out to the wagon.

"I suppose we'll find out about the trip little by little," Mother said. "Henry can tell long yarns, but he never will tell about a trip when he first comes home. That is his Indian nature, I guess. Sometimes his French blood is on top and then he talks and talks."

"Jack is very provoking too," his mother said. "I tell him I have to dig for any information I get."

Before long the three were back with the canoe and all it had held. Aunt Ellen was excited because there were so many ducks and geese; Mother said the feathers would be fine to have. Henry was satisfied with nineteen big salmon that he could salt down. Jack said he guessed he'd learned a lot, but he wished he could have shot a deer.

After supper the travelers did tell a few stories. One worried Aunt Ellen. Jack told about the second night when they camped in a shack that belonged to Prater, a friend of Henry's. No one was at home, but they found plenty of dry wood; that was what they needed to dry their clothes, for they had been in the rain all day—and hadn't caught a thing but salmon, Jack added with disgust.

They cooked supper and stretched out by the fire to sleep, glad that they had a shelter, for the rain was pouring and the wind blowing. Jack said that he dreamed in the night that he was swimming, and woke to find that the rain was pouring in a stream down the chimney. When daylight came they found that the top of the chimney, which was made of clay and sticks, had softened and blown off even with the edge of the roof.

"So the roof made a good thing to catch the rain and pour it on us," Henry finished. "We started out the next

162

day almost as wet as when we got there. The next night we stopped at an Indian lodge——"

"Honestly?" Aunt Ellen was surprised.

"Yes, ma'am, you know I'm part Indian," Henry said.

"That was one night we were dry and didn't have to cook our supper." Jack spoke up quickly; Abby thought he was afraid that his mother had hurt Henry's feelings. "There was a big fire in the middle of the room and we wrapped up in our blankets around that."

"You've heard of old Mac, Will. One night we slept in the old zinc shack he used to live in. Had to have our fire outdoors, but I had gathered wild parsnips that day and we had a good fire near the door, so we cooked easily."

"I don't understand about wild parsnips and a fire," Uncle John said.

"These were the stalks, I meant. They are hollow and have a kind of resin inside that is always dry—best thing to start wet wood."

"Speaking of fire . . ." Jack turned to Abby and said in a loud voice, *"Chako, hiac! Wohksa claagepah!"*

She grinned and shook her head. *"Wake!"* she told him. Then she said to Henry, pointing to Jack, *"Tenas tilicum, hiyu pelton, cultus wawa."*

"Shucks," Jack groaned, "I learned those Chehalis words because I thought you didn't know them."

"I'll be honest," Abby said. "I didn't understand the last part. But I knew you said 'Come, quick!' and that by your tone you were trying to boss me. What was the other thing you said?"

163

Jack was mollified. " 'Wohksa claagepah' means 'Get some wood.' "

"I'll remember that," Abby said. "Do you know what I said?"

"Yes. 'Your little friend is foolish, talks nonsense.' "

"Good!" Abby praised him. "I'm glad that you can learn even if you don't like school."

Henry told Mother he had brought a piece of sturgeon and that he would like to cook it for dinner the next day.

"If it's anything like that salmon, I'm in favor," Uncle John said. "How did you get just a piece of sturgeon, not the whole fish?"

"We-ell," Henry said, "I didn't catch it; an Indian friend of mine gave it to me. And the whole fish weighed more than three hundred pounds. Too much sturgeon."

Jack yawned. "I have to get those four otter and the coon skinned and ready for Mr. Lum, so I must get up early. I'd like to see what it feels like to sleep dry again." He got up, then reached in his pocket as if he had almost forgotten something. He gave a small package to Abby. "Here are some tiny shells I picked up; odd-shaped, I thought. If you'd like it, I'll make you a little box some-day and we can glue these on the lid." He walked out before Abby could thank him.

Abby put the shells carefully by her Queen Susan box on the mantel. She had begun to worry for fear Jack had come back from the trip disliking the rain and the Terri-tory more than ever. But as she thought it over, she de-cided that he was more cheerful than usual.

164

CHAPTER **Ten**

In spite of going to bed happy on Monday, Tuesday everybody got out of the wrong side of bed. Henry told Mother that he couldn't cook the sturgeon as he had promised, for the bacon was ready to smoke and he had to clean the salmon ready to smoke or dry. Jack wanted to help Henry and after that he was going to run his traps. So neither of them would help with the regular chores. Uncle John rode to the mill after he had worked a while.

Clara had a cold and was cross because Abby refused to read a story to her.

"I can't play with you, Baby, I have work to do. Father has been left alone with the chores; I'm going to help him." Abby was out of humor since Mother couldn't carry out her plan of going up to the store to get Mrs. Browning's help in cutting the blue dress. As usual, Abby thought, all the other work comes first, and if there is any time for me, all right.

Dinner didn't start out pleasantly. Everyone was late and that always irritated Mother. "The least folks can do is to come to eat when I get things ready," she said.

Father came in first, then Uncle John, as they were sitting down. "Henry said not to worry about him; he wants to finish a stint he's set and he can rustle his own grub," Father said.

"Where is Jack?" Aunt Ellen asked.

"He's running his traps in the woods; we'd better not wait."

Nobody was cheerful, but the roast ducks tasted good, so they ate. There was winter squash, and beets that Aunt Ellen cooked with a sweet-sour sauce. We always eat, Abby thought.

Henry came in and ate quickly in one of his silent spells.

They had almost finished dinner when they heard running in the yard. The next instant there was a thud as something heavy hit the side of the house. Before anyone could speak, Jack rushed in. Blood was streaming from his face; his coat sleeve was ripped, and they could see blood running from a gash in his arm.

Aunt Ellen screamed, but Jack didn't say a word. He grabbed his arrows from the mantel and ran out again. The family pushed outside in time to see him shoot an arrow into the head of a small bear that was lying against the house.

As Jack fumbled to get another arrow, Father put his arm around him and said, "That bear's dead, Jack. Come in the house so we can get this bleeding stopped."

Aunt Ellen was crying so much she couldn't help. Mother kept her out of the way, and the men worked with Jack.

Uncle John took charge, and Abby was proud of him;

he certainly knew exactly what to do. She brought basins of water, and rags.

Before very long Jack was sitting up in the big bed, his face white. His right arm and shoulder were wrapped in a big roll of bandages, so Aunt Ellen held the cup while he drank coffee.

They all stood around asking questions.

"Neat job, young feller, killing that bear even when your arm was clawed," Henry said. "But how did you happen to have him down here alive?"

"I started running the traps from the far end, like you told me," Jack said. "A cougar was in the first one. I didn't aim very well and I had to use three arrows before I killed him. I saw a deer in the brush and used three arrows trying to get him—no luck. When I came to the last trap, here was this bear, but all my arrows were gone. Lucky there was a broken tree branch near and I clubbed the bear senseless with that. I dragged the cougar into the brush—I had dragged him that far—and then I put the bear over my back to bring him here to kill him."

Jack stopped to drink more coffee and rest a minute.

"Well, I was hurrying down the trail, 'bout a mile from here I guess, when I felt that bear moving on my back! He had come to! Before I could throw him, he had clawed my face and gashed my arm."

Aunt Ellen began to cry again. "He might have killed you!"

"Maybe, but he didn't, and next time I'll know enough

to hit a bear harder. We wrastled, and finally I knocked his head against a stump and then carried him down here. Say, Mother, I'm hungry as a bear. I haven't had any dinner; can't I have something to eat?"

"Guess you'll make out all right from here on," Uncle John said. "I'll give him some coffee while you bring a plate of grub, Ellen."

"I'm going after that cougar," Henry said. "Is he near that last trap we set?"

"Oh, thanks, Henry, I sure don't want to lose him. Yes, he's in the brush under a big fir. Bet he's nine feet long."

"I'll find it," Henry assured him. "Say, Jack, you'll be thinking you're the smartest hunter in Lewis County—a cat and a bear all in one day!"

Jack shook his head, but winced as if the motion hurt. "I didn't get a deer, and I was counting on giving Abby a job cooking it for me."

"Things seem to be going all right in here," Father said. "I'll take the bear and hang him in the barn, then I'd better go with you, Henry, to get that cat—if he's as big as Jack thinks!"

While Aunt Ellen fed Jack, Mother and Abby cleared the table and did the other work. Abby went upstairs to clean her room—and saw the blue wool goods. Suddenly she knew what this accident would mean to her.

Even if Jack didn't have to stay in bed—and he was already saying he would be up for supper—he wouldn't be able to work hard for a long time since he couldn't use his right arm. Aunt Ellen would fuss around over him; she wouldn't be much help to Mother. Abby knew without anyone telling her that there was no chance for the Olympia trip with the Brownings next week.

Worse still, Aunt Ellen would decide that she wouldn't stay in a country where there were storms and wild animals, that was certain. Then Abby would have to stay home until Clara was big enough to help Mother. And I'll be so old I won't want to go to school. At the thought, she threw herself on the bed and cried and cried.

Finally, when there didn't seem to be another tear to squeeze out, she sat up and held the blue goods around her as if it were a dress. She tried to play her favorite "all-alone" game and make up a story where she was the heroine. "Our heroine bravely tried to smile. Life had not been kind; Fate struck one blow after another . . ." She began to cry again. There was no use pretending, she didn't want to feel better; she didn't want to smile.

Jack had been plain careless, and now he sat up in bed and acted like he thought he was a hero. Everybody would wait on him and spoil him. It wasn't fair; nothing was fair.

Still, she decided, there was no use being mean to Mother; it wasn't her fault. Abby smoothed the goods— did tears spot wool, she wondered—wrapped it carefully, and went slowly downstairs.

"Mother, will you put this away for me until Christmas? Then it will seem like a new present. I'm growing so fast you'd better not make it up for a year or so. I won't likely be going on any trip—ever." She choked. "Shall I ride over this afternoon and tell Mrs. Browning that I can't go to Olympia with them?"

Her mother stopped kneading the bread and kissed her. "Yes, Abigail; you are a very good girl. But there'll be some other time."

Good, am I! Abby thought as she pulled on her outdoor clothes. If being mean would do any good, you'd see. She hurried out. "Another thing," she muttered, "no pets to talk to now except that silly old Tilly." She kicked some branches out of her way, and the end of one flew up and hit her face. Even that! Kloshe nickered when he heard her coming. She put her arms around his neck and cried a little. "You understand me," she whispered.

She was wiping her eyes when Uncle John came by. He looked at her a minute and then asked, "You are only thirteen years old, aren't you, Abby?"

"Going on fourteen."

"You can't teach before you are sixteen, can you?"

"Yes, I heard of one teacher who taught at fifteen."

"Say fifteen, then. That's plenty of time. Now, this is what I had in mind: we'll have time for lessons this winter, and some in the spring and summer."

"If you stay." Abby was mournful.

"And then when you go away to school you can take some examinations and you'll catch up with those that are older than you."

"If I ever do go away."

"Abby, what was the name of that teacher you liked so well?"

"Miss Peebles; why?"

"Did she expect you to have your lessons without studying, or tell you that things happened without working, and sometimes waiting?"

"No . . . Oh, Uncle John, you think that I haven't enough patience to be a good teacher! Oh, dear." She wiped her eyes.

"Patience is one thing you must learn, just like arithmetic. You are the only one who can teach yourself that. Remind me to read you a poem that says, 'Patience is power.' If you study, you'll find that examinations are easy."

"But I can't go away and leave Mother alone. . . ."

Her uncle gave her a shake. "There you go, feeling sorry for yourself and worrying. You are silly. If you were forty years old and there was no chance for you ever to go away to school, there might be some sense in your worrying."

Abby had to laugh. Her uncle had never scolded her before. "I'll be good." She led Kloshe and they walked up the path as they talked. Uncle John went on.

"You should have learned patience, working on a farm. Do you put eggs under a hen and expect chickens to hatch the next day? Or do you plant things and then dig up the seeds to see whether they are growing?"

They both laughed so hard that Mother came to the door and saw them.

"This is the first day of the Watson-Conner University," Uncle John explained. "We have book lessons to-night."

Mother smiled. "I must say it didn't sound like school to me. Abby, you'd better get started now. If you hurry, you'll have time to ride on to Mr. Lum's. Jack wants you to tell him about the cougar. You can stop at Browning's on your way home."

The ride, and thinking about Uncle John's talk, made Abby feel better. At any rate, it would be fun to study with him. Even if the Watsons didn't decide to stay out West, she was glad she had had her uncle this winter. He might scold, but he always saw her side of things.

Mr. Lum was home, and was much interested in her story. "Jack wants the bearskin for himself, but he'd like to sell the cougar to you. I suppose he wants a bear rug so he can point to it and tell how brave he is!"

He shook his head at her. "Abby, you said you wanted your cousin to be happy, and now you are cross when he is proud of what he has done. That isn't like you. Jack is a fine boy, I think, and I'm sure he'll get along fine out here. Tell Henry to bring me both the animals; I'll have time to skin them and cure the hides. This is the right time of year to get fur; it's thick, ready for winter. And tell Jack that I'll buy his cougar, and see that he gets a bounty, too."

Abby found Mrs. Browning and Nettie in the kitchen. She was feeling hungry and gladly took a big piece of the apple pie that was hot from the oven. She decided

172

to make a good story of Jack's adventure and made him quite a hero. "But it means that I won't be able to go to Olympia with you. I'm awful sorry, but of course, Jack won't be able to work for a couple of weeks, and he'll need waiting on, too."

"The poor boy!" Nettie said. "I'll have to go down and visit him and cheer him up."

"Jack doesn't like visitors." Abby didn't try to be polite. She carefully scraped up the last bite and put on her cape. "I must hurry; I'll have to help with the chores."

"I'm sorry, Abby, that you can't go, but there will be some other time," Mrs. Browning said. "When the railroad comes through the Flats, maybe next spring, we'll go often to Olympia to visit."

Abby growled to herself as she rode home. People like to say, "There'll be some other time." How do they know? However, she suddenly realized that she was singing, "There's No Place Like Home." She laughed, and by the time she went in to see Jack she was almost happy.

She reported what Mr. Lum had said. "Henry plans to take the animals first thing in the morning."

"Thanks, Abby. You do understand how a fellow feels." He hesitated, as if he had something special to tell her. "By the way, Father and I had a talk this afternoon . . ." He was sitting by the fireplace; they had been alone, but now Mother came in to look at the bread she was baking. "Never mind," Jack went on, "I'll tell you some other time."

173

Abby went out glumly to get some bark that Mother wanted. She was sure what Jack wanted to tell her. He and his mother had talked things over and had decided that they wouldn't stay in the Territory. Remembering her new rule not to worry was going to be hard, she saw.

Aunt Ellen was happy when Mother began planning for Thanksgiving. "Let me help, Julia," she said. "I am excited to think that this year we will be with relatives. That is the way this day should be spent, I think."

Mother kissed her. "Yes, this is a family day. Of course, I'm counting on your help, Ellen."

"Thanksgiving is the most important holiday New Englanders have, Abby," Aunt Ellen said. "You remember from your history that the Pilgrims started the custom in Massachusetts. Different villages in New England always observed it, and other colonies took it up. George Washington wanted it for the whole country, but if it hadn't been for a woman, Thanksgiving might never have been observed nationally."

"A woman?" Abby was interested.

Uncle grinned. "Listen to your aunt and you'll find out that women are very important people."

"This woman is important. You remember that magazine, *Godey's Lady's Book*, that you were looking through for a pattern? She is the editor. For almost twenty years she wrote editorials, urging that Thanksgiving be observed all over the United States. She wrote over and over to four different presidents when they were in office.

174

Finally, she convinced President Lincoln and he proclaimed it a national day of Thanksgiving. And a New England woman was responsible."

Father tried to look worried. "If you have finished your lecture, Mrs. Watson, may I ask what we are going to eat to show that we are thankful?"

"Turkey and venison, potatoes, squash, onions, dried corn, cabbage, mince pies, bread, preserves, pickles——" Mother recited as if this were a lesson she had learned by heart.

"Whoa!" Father said. He went to the mantel and picked up the almanac. "Let's see, we'll probably eat about one o'clock. That means there are ten days and eighteen hours to wait for that dinner. Please don't tell us any more. And don't starve us until then."

"Ten days will give you time to get the turkey a little fatter and to get a deer so we'll have some venison," Mother said. "We have everything else right here. Ellen even has the mincemeat ready. She used the neck of that deer Henry brought in. I won't starve you, but I have enough work planned to keep up your appetite."

Funny how things work out, Abby thought. I was brokenhearted when I didn't get to go to Olympia with the Brownings. If I had gone, I would have missed the fun we have had these evenings. Uncle John is right, I guess; a person should go on and do the work for each day and not worry. I'll explain that to my school children.

Her uncle had unpacked his violin a few days before and now was playing softly on it. Henry and Jack were at the table, absorbed in a game of checkers. Mother's spinning wheel and the crackling of the fire added to the pleasant noises. Abby picked up her Towne's speller and her slate. Bet she'd know those words the next time she was asked.

Mother stood up and put her spinning wheel away. "There. I wanted to get that much yarn ready for tomorrow. Ellen and I are spending the day with Mrs. Davis, and I'll need the yarn for my knitting."

"I've been planning to do some work at Gordon's blacksmith shop," Father said. "He told me I could bring up the tools that need repair. I'll take you two ladies in the wagon, if I may?" Father bowed to them.

"I promised to go to the mill tomorrow to work on their books," Uncle John said. "I'd like to ride with you, Will."

"Abby, with all of us gone, there won't be much cooking to do. I'll put up lunches for the men. Could you do some of the washing?" Mother asked. "If you'll look after things here tomorrow, you can have the next two days off to do as you please."

Jack looked up from his whittling. Although his arm was bandaged, he could use his hand very well and he was making some stirring spoons for his mother from an old broken whiffletree. "Remember I'll be here for dinner, Aunt Julia."

"I can cook up something for us, young feller," Henry said.

As soon as the breakfast work was done the next morning, the family left. Even Clara begged at the last minute to go, so her mother took her.

"I'm going out to run the traps," Henry said. "I won't be gone long."

Abby laughed. "If Henry gets out in the woods, he may be gone until afternoon. He never knows how time is going when he's out there. I'll put some clothes to boil in the kettle in the yard; it's a good chance, with this sunshine. I'll get our dinner, don't worry, Jack."

Two hours later Henry had not come back. Abby started potatoes to boil and then sat down by the fire to rest. "I'll get meat and other things in a few minutes."

Jack was working on fish nets for Henry and they both sat silently. Suddenly Abby giggled. We are sitting by the fire like an old married couple, she thought.

Jack looked at her as if he knew her mind and she felt her face turn red. "Guess I'll get dinner on the table." She got up from her stool.

"Wait," Jack said. "You know I told you the other day I had a talk with Father?"

Abby's heart went down, plunk, plunk. "Yes," she answered, sure that he would say that Uncle John had agreed that they should leave in the spring.

"Well, it was partly about you. I know I'm only fifteen, and you are just thirteen . . ."

"Going on fourteen."

"Anyway, out West, I've heard, people start early to think about having a home. I mean . . . Well—I wish you'd promise not to think about any other boy for three years. By that time I'll have work somewhere, I'm sure."

"I'll be teaching then."

"So you've said a thousand times! Maybe you'll be going away to school and you'll meet lots of new young folks. Anyway, don't promise any boy anything without telling me first. Remember, I'm not actually your cousin."

"But maybe you'll not be around here."

"You can write letters."

Abby thought a minute. "It all sounds queer, but if it will make you any happier, I can promise that I'll tell you what I plan to do before I do it."

"That's not much of a promise, but it's something. Now I'll tell you what I'm going to do. I talked it over with Father, but we decided to wait until after Thanksgiving to tell Mother. When we were in Olympia, Henry and I went by the Crosby mill in Tumwater. They said I could have a job there after Christmas. The mill is getting logs in, fast, and there will be work sawing. I'll get my board and some money."

"Oh, Jack, that's fine! I am glad."

"Humph, I didn't think you'd say that. You are always talking about how much you want me to stay here, and now you are glad to hear that I am leaving."

"Tumwater isn't very far away; you can come back here often. The thing is that means that Uncle John and Aunt Ellen will stay here."

"You'd rather have them around than me. I see."

"Jack, don't be silly. They are teaching me so that I can go to school and then take my teacher's examinations. That is the most important thing in my life." She was looking out the window and was glad to see Henry coming; that would stop this argument. "Listen, there's Henry; I must put dinner on."

Henry opened the door with a bang. "Got us a deer! That much for our Thanksgiving dinner." He talked so much while they ate that he didn't seem to notice that Jack wasn't very gay. However, when Henry said that there were some land otter and a beaver in Jack's traps, he was happier.

During the next few days Abby thought often about what Jack had said. He acted older when he talked that way. Evidently Mother was right; he wasn't going to be any good as a playmate. But now she was busy with schoolwork and didn't care to play.

She was glad he was going to work at the mill. That would give him money and make him like the West better. He told her that he had earned over eighteen dollars with his traps, and seemed almost grown-up when he talked about earning money to take care of his father and mother. Funny notion that he had, to take the responsibility for her, too. Well, if it made him any happier to think he could plan for her, all right. These lessons made her feel older; she would plan for herself.

One thing, sure, there was no use telling Nettie Browning that Jack was going to work at Tumwater. Nettie would probably try to finagle a chance to go to school in Olympia, or at least to make a long visit there. And that was across the little bay, practically in Tumwater.

Of course, if Jack worked there for a year and Abby could go to school in Olympia—but there was no use planning so far ahead.

Father said that there were some single men that he would like to invite for Thanksgiving dinner, so finally there were a dozen people crowded around the table. Crowding made it all the more jolly.

Every kind of food Mother had planned, and more, was on the table. They ate and ate until everyone was stuffed. Father said that it might be a good idea to rest up and tell some stories before dessert came on; then they could eat more.

The men moved over around the fire while the women cleared the table and brought pie and cake, cider and coffee.

One of the men had been mining on the Fraser River, so he told them stories about Canada.

Captain Dunbar had been on a ship that ran aground between San Francisco and Portland. Then he told about crossing the bar at the mouth of the Columbia River, where many ships had been stuck and then pounded to pieces by the waves. A cove at the entrance was named Graveyard Cove; so many wrecks had piled up there.

"Why don't they run a steamer on the Chehalis River?" Uncle John asked. "Unless my geography is wrong, a boat could get close to Olympia and save driving over these roads that everyone says are so bad. Be an easy way to get stock there, wouldn't it?"

180

"Right," Captain Dunbar said. "As a matter of fact, I ran a little steamer on the Chehalis River, three, four years ago. Used to go down to the mouth of the Black River, then up the Black to 'bout ten miles from Olympia and people packed in from there. Didn't pay, got stuck on mud bars. I mind how we finally caught on to running the steamer backward when we struck shallow water."

Uncle John laughed. "I'm sure there is a joke in this, but I'll ask: How did that help you?"

"Well, you see, 'twas a stern-wheeler. So when we ran it backwards, it threw the water under and lifted her up. T'other way, took the water out from under."

"Henry, that sounds like one of your yarns," Aunt Ellen said.

"Beg pardon, ma'am, but this is true." Captain Dunbar looked at her without even smiling. "The Chehalis is an unusual river. Hard to navigate, but a fine river. Not many streams can run up and down at once, same channel."

Uncle John protested. "Now, Captain Dunbar, just because we are from the East——"

"Fact. Seen it lots of times. Down at the mouth. High tide backs the water up one side of the channel, river runs down the other!"

After they had eaten pie and other things, Mr. Morgan pointed at the mantel. "I've been looking at that fiddle. Who plays? Can't we have some music?"

So Uncle John played and they all sang. There was "Listen to the Mocking Bird," "The Gum Tree Canoe,"

"Do They Miss Me at Home?" While they were resting, Henry surprised them by singing a mournful cowboy tune, "Oh, bury me not on the lone prairee . . ."

"Well," said Uncle John, "if you want to be mournful . . ." He played and sang:

> "Oh, the hinges are of leather,
> And the windows have no glass,
> And the board roof lets the howling blizzard in;
> And I hear the hungry coyote,
> As he slinks up through the grass,
> Round my little old sod shanty on my claim!"

When the visitors left, telling Mother that they wouldn't be able to eat for a week, they were so full, the family got to work. The men went out to the chores, and the women cleared the food away and washed the dishes

Mother left enough on the table so that if anyone wanted to eat before they went to bed, they could help themselves.

Aunt Ellen was happy. "It's been a wonderful day! After all these years, Abby, we've had Thanksgiving together."

"The next thing to plan is Christmas," Abby announced. "There's going to be a program at the church. Mr. Stearns—he runs the Sunday school, you remember, Uncle John, is getting up a program. He said he wanted you to play something on your violin. Mrs. Browning is helping him and she promised to ask you the next time you came to the store, but I said I would put the idea in your mind. Will you, Uncle John?"

"Why, perhaps, if you are sure they want me. . . ."

"Abby, the Arranger," Father said.

"Well, if you don't plan for things, how do you get them? I hope we plan for just a family Christmas, though, for Jack——" She stopped, for she remembered that Aunt Ellen didn't know that Jack was going away to work.

"What do you want for a present, Abby?" Aunt Ellen asked. "I know you wouldn't ask for something impossible."

"*Klonas.* That's jargon for 'I don't know,'" she told Jack. "But I do know; I want a geography."

"John, do you remember old Sloane's horse?" Father asked.

Uncle John laughed. "Yes, and I think I see your point."

"I don't know that story," said Henry.

"Well, for about ten years the Sloanes lived on a little farm near Middlebury, then they moved farther away. But whenever they came to town, the horse would never pass the old farm without turning in. He would stop at the gate, and balk. So the Sloanes learned to drive into the yard, go to the barn, stop, turn around, and the horse would jog off happily to town. I was thinking that's like Abby. No matter what conversational road you start on, she has to stop at school for a minute!"

Abby winked at her father. "Let's talk about Christmas!"

CHAPTER **Eleven**

Jack took the chance at breakfast the next morning, when everyone was there, to tell about his job. "I'm glad that I didn't promise to go earlier. I knew that you would want me here for the holidays, Mother; now, with my arm hurt, I couldn't have gone."

Aunt Ellen looked proud and worried at the same time, Abby thought. Mother said she thought it was fine that Jack had found work that way.

"Are you sure you are old enough, Jack?" his mother asked. "I don't mean just for the work, you are as strong as a man, but . . ."

"Best way for him to learn is to get out and do," Father said. "He won't come to harm."

"I had hoped there would be work close here," Aunt Ellen began.

"Please don't worry, Mother." Jack's voice showed that he was trying to be patient.

Aunt Ellen was quiet a minute, then she smiled. "I always knew I never could be like a robin and push my youngster out of the nest to learn to fly. Well, what clothes will you need?"

"He'd better buy them in Olympia, Ellen," Uncle John said. "Will tells me that the stores there have special

185

logging clothes. I can let Jack have the money he needs."

"I'll pay you back, Father," Jack said quickly. "But, Mother, I was thinking that if you would knit me some socks . . ."

Aunt Ellen got up from the table. "I'll get at them right now. Julia, you said that I could have some of that home-spun yarn of yours. Could you get it now?"

Her needles were clicking rapidly the next few days. Abby had fretted a bit when the idea of making socks came up, for Aunt Ellen had promised to rip up the silk dress she had shown the women the day of the party and make new dresses for Clara and Abby. However, her aunt had not forgotten, and told Abby that she could help rip the dress if she would be very careful. Mother helped, and pressed the folds of silk ready. By the end of a week, there were three pairs of socks pressed and put away.

"That's enough, Mother," Jack told her. "Remember I have some old socks; I haven't been going barefoot, you know. I don't want more stuff than I can carry in a blanket roll."

Mother and Aunt Ellen spent one afternoon at the store and Mrs. Browning helped cut the two dresses. Then Abby rode to the Washingtons' and they did all the long seams on the machine. In another week, the finishing was done and the two dresses hung ready for the Christmas program. Every morning Clara asked hopefully whether that was the night they would dress up.

"I wish that man that came around taking pictures on Ford's Prairie and Boisfort last year would come here," Abby said. "I'd like to have pictures of us in these beautiful dresses. I could pay for them out of that money I saved for the Olympia trip. Like as not, I won't get to go there for a long time—if ever." She saw Uncle John laughing and stopped.

"Didn't you cross one bridge this week before you got there, Abby?" he asked. "I thought you were worrying about Jack's socks taking so long you wouldn't get a new dress—but you did get it!"

"I know, I know," Abby muttered. "'Patience is power,' but I believe in going out and getting things myself."

Knitting and sewing were put away a week or so before Christmas. The rest of the time was spent cooking and planning how to make the cabin festive. On Saturday Jack and the girls hunted for a small tree that had a pretty shape but wouldn't take too much room.

"Don't get a hemlock," Father said. "Those needles fall too quickly. Better make a small box, Jack, put some stones in the bottom to hold it steady, then get wet moss and pack it around the tree. We can pour some water on once in a while, and the tree won't dry out."

After they had that done, Jack and Abby gathered some rose hips down the road from the old Davis cabin. The briar roses had been planted there for twenty years and this summer the flowers had been thick so there were lots of the big red berry seed pods. After supper

187

they strung these and popped corn for the white strings. Father surprised them with some picture cards he had brought from Olympia. He showed them how to fasten them at the corner with black threads that didn't show, so the cards twirled around when a draft came through the room.

Henry was away for a week, but came back the Sunday before Christmas. He hadn't said where he was going, only that he supposed he would have to stay home in January if Jack went away, so he was getting in a trip. They found that he had gone to Portland and back by Willapa Harbor. He brought some tiny oysters that Aunt Ellen made into a savory stew, but what Abby liked best was an orange for each of them. She put the oranges in a row on the mantel because the color was so pretty. That seemed to need a background, so she gathered cedar that had tiny cones and set a bouquet of them in a can in the center.

Uncle John practiced some songs to play at the program, and taught the girls an old English song, "The First Nowel." He played the air very softly while they sang so that they wouldn't lose the tune. Clara felt very important, and drove Abby nearly wild asking every morning how long it would be until the program.

"Listen, Baby," Abby said while they were making the long strings of popcorn, "you can count to five. Today is Saturday and Christmas is on Wednesday. Counting today, that is five days. The program will be the evening of the fourth day. Here, put five sticks in the corner where you keep your dolls. Every day take one away."

Monday morning at breakfast Clara said, "Today is Christmas."

"No, Clara," Mother said, "there are two more days."

Clara wailed. "But the sticks are all gone! I throwed them in the fire so today would be Christmas!"

"Clara!" Abby was impatient, but when she saw Uncle John smiling she laughed. She tried to mimic her uncle's voice. " 'Patience is power,' little girl. Come on, let's sing our song; tomorrow night we have to sing it to a lot of people."

The little church was crowded for the program the night before Christmas. Not only were there the people who lived at Claquato, and below the hill, by the river, but some came from Boisfort, and even from as far as Cutting's Prairie and Saunders' Flats. There were teams tied to the hitching posts and to the maples, all down the street.

The women set the tables in Pearson's carpenter shop and loaded them with loaves of bread, cold meats, pies and cakes. That morning Aunt Ellen took a butter mold from her trunk. "I was going to give you this tomorrow, Julia, but perhaps you would like to use it for the plate of butter you are taking tonight."

She set the hinged wooden form on the table; Abby saw that it had the figure of a cow inside.

"Please, Mother, may I try it?"

Her mother agreed and Abby went to work. The first time she didn't have the mold cold and wet enough, but then she learned, and made two perfect little cows that they took to the party table.

"We had a Swiss neighbor in Kansas who made it for me," Aunt Ellen explained in answer to questions.

Mr. Browning put plates of candy on the table; he had sent clear to Victoria to get a special kind that came from England.

When the tables were ready, everyone gathered in the little church. There were so many that they crowded clear out on the porch.

Mr. Stearns read the Christmas story from the Bible, and there were songs, first by everyone, then by the Sunday school. Uncle John played the tune on his violin; it sounded very nice with the organ.

Abby felt a little sad when the school children spoke pieces. She wanted to grow up, but she wanted to be a pupil with the others. It was too bad that a person had to choose, and couldn't have everything, she thought.

At last it was time for the duet and Clara surprised her family by remembering the words and singing clearly. As soon as they finished, Clara made the audience laugh. She took Abby's hand and said, "Now, let's go over to Pearson's and get our candy." Abby had a hard time convincing her that the program wasn't over.

Soon, though, they were at the party. The two girls walked around so that their new dresses could be admired. The women who had seen the dress at the quilting kept telling Aunt Ellen how nicely she had made them.

The party was fun; they played games at one side

where Mr. Pearson had pushed the lumber back. Abby didn't want to play rough ones for fear her dress would be torn, but drop the handkerchief and London Bridge were all right.

Someone asked for square dancing, so the children stood back and watched eight couples going through the steps. Uncle John played "Old Dan Tucker" and "The Girl I Left Behind Me," and called the steps, too.

Abby was proud to think that in three months her relatives had made so many friends. Her aunt and uncle were talking to people as if they had known them for years. Jack, however, stood back against the wall with the other boys of his age. They didn't dance, and they hadn't played any games. Feel too big, Abby thought. Oh well, there was no use worrying about Jack.

She was glad when everyone was ready to go home. Clara had gone to sleep and didn't wake up until they were home again.

"Time for presents?" she asked hopefully.

The presents were to wait until morning, but Abby thought that Christmas Eve with just the family around the fire was the nicest part of the holiday. Clara insisted on singing the duet with Abby again. Then they all sang songs, some old and some new ones. Uncle John nearly always had a new one to teach them. The tree, they all agreed, was the prettiest they had ever seen.

Although Abby woke early, she smelled breakfast cooking, and whispered to Clara, "Come on, Baby, now it's time for presents."

Mother let them open their presents and eat breakfast at the same time. There was such a hubbub as they admired each other's gifts that it sounded like a party with lots of people.

After Clara looked at her present from Aunt Ellen, she went back in her corner and paid no attention to the rest of the family. It was a doll that Aunt Ellen had been given when she was a little girl. The face was wax, and was almost like skin, and the hair was in beautiful curls. Father gave her a little bed he had made; Mother had fitted it with quilts and pillows. That was the first store doll Clara had ever owned, and she could hardly talk or eat the rest of the day.

Abby wasn't sure which of her presents she liked best. At her place at the table she found a very tiny package; she couldn't think what could be so small. The others were watching as she shook it and felt it. Jack was impatient. "Open it," he said.

She found a gold locket and chain. Inside was a picture.

"That's your grandmother Conner," Father said. "When we wrote that we were giving you the locket, she sent the picture. 'From one Abigail to another,' she said." He looked at the picture a long time; Abby knew he was wishing he could see his mother.

"The locket was given me on my fourteenth birthday," Mother told her. "I've been saving it for tomorrow, when you would be fourteen, but I decided to give it to you for Christmas."

Father patted her cheek. "Poor Abby, with a birthday right after Christmas, nobody pays any attention to how old she is."

"I'll be practically grown-up tomorrow, whether anybody notices it or not," Abby said. She laid the locket against the blue goods that Father had given her. "This will be beautiful with either the blue dress or my new silk one," Abby said. "This is a Christmas I'll always remember."

Her present from Jack was a small chest that she knew would fit under her bedroom window. She could sit on it and look at the trees and the sunsets. He had made leather hinges for it, and carved her name on the lid. In it she could put her schoolbooks and the new Christmas ones.

Henry gave her a book he bought in Portland. "This is an old book, Abby, printed before you were born, but I thought you'd like to read it maybe better than some new one. It's about California and the forty-niners, they told me." He didn't like to say he could read very little.

"*Incidents on Land and Water, or Four Years on the Pacific Coast*," Abby read. "By a Mrs. Bates. Henry, thank you very much! Maybe I can read it out loud in the evening to everybody."

Henry didn't answer, but she saw him smile a little. He was very busy with his cooking. A week before he had asked Mother whether he could have a goose for Christmas dinner. "My father said it was a French-Canadian custom to have it for Christmas; I'll cook it the way he

193

taught my mother." He had it already cleaned and stuffed and soon after breakfast he put it on a spit that he had fashioned for the fireplace. All morning, while the others were talking and looking at their presents, he was turning the goose and watching it slowly brown.

Once Jack found a chance to whisper to Abby. "While I'm away I'll think of how good that goose smelled and the sputter of the grease falling into the fire. Maybe I'm getting homesick. Don't forget what I told you a month ago; you're my girl, and you must tell me all your plans."

Abby said "All right," but she wasn't paying much attention. She was reading from the book of Longfellow's poems that was Uncle John's present to her.

"I wish you'd listen to me," he said.

At dinner they all tried to be very gay, so that Aunt Ellen wouldn't remember that Jack was leaving in two days. Mother had said that they wouldn't invite any company; that a family party would be nicer. From the goose, cooked to a turn, as they told Henry, to the plum pudding Mother boiled in a sack and served hot with a hard sauce, the feast was good.

"I'm glad that Abby isn't eating much," Jack said. "That shows that she feels bad about my going away, even if she does say mean things about me."

Abby laughed. "I'm so chock-full of happiness that there isn't any room for food. Oh, I don't mean happiness because you are going away, Jack! But so many nice things are happening to me—two new dresses and my books and a locket . . . And tomorrow I'm fourteen."

194

Her birthday felt like a very special day, although she had only one gift. It was wonderful to be fourteen; somehow that seemed very grown-up. She made lots of new resolutions: now she was so old she wouldn't cry about little things; she wouldn't be cross with Clara; she would help with the chores even when she would rather go riding, or to her hide-out. She thought perhaps she should wait to see how she kept those before she made any more.

Her feelings were all mixed up; she was glad that she had a chance to study, but she was sorry that Jack was going to be away; he was getting very friendly.

Henry gave her the only special birthday present. While he was in Portland he had gone into a Chinese laundry. "I like Chinese," Henry said. "They don't make as much fuss about being smart as lots of white people do, but they know things." The Chinese took him into his own room and made tea for him. Henry saw some little Chinese figures showing tea drinkers and he persuaded the laundryman to sell them. "I heard you say you wanted to travel to China," he told Abby, "so I knew you would like these."

He was too surprised to move when Abby threw her arms around him. "Oh, Henry, thanks! This is a real grown-up present, just right for my fourteenth birthday."

In the afternoon Jack asked her to ride to Mr. Lum's with him. He wanted to talk about the furs that he had trapped and to tell Mr. Lum that he was going away.

When they came to the level place at the foot of the

hill, Abby suggested a race. They laughed, remembering that first afternoon when they had gone to Mr. Lum's and Abby had beat Jack in a race. Now he knew how to ride and let the reins hang loose on Skookum's neck. The two ponies went at the same rate, and came to the ferry together.

"You've changed your ideas about how to ride," Abby said.

"I've changed my ideas about lots of things in three months," Jack replied.

Mr. Lum was glad to see them and said they must come in and have some of his Christmas cake. He handed Abby a book. "I wanted to get this to you for a sort of Christmas present, but I couldn't," he said. "You always talk about reading, so I sent for this, *David Copperfield* by Charles Dickens. You can have a good time crying over this!"

"Thanks very much, Mr. Lum. Today is my birthday, I'm fourteen, so this is a present for that. Henry gave me one, and it was a sort of grown-up present too."

"I went up in the woods this morning and sprung all my traps, Mr. Lum," Jack said. "I'm going to Tumwater tomorrow to work in the mill. Maybe Henry would be too busy or away somewhere, so he couldn't see to the traps. I wouldn't like to think of animals in them starving to death."

"That's right, Jack. Soon as I get the money for the furs I sent in, I'll give it to Abby. Want to see your bear rug? It's almost cured, but I'm going to get glass eyes in and

196

line the skin with cloth before I give it to you for a rug. Be careful in the mill," he called as they rode away. "Not a very safe place, you know."

Abby began to worry as they rode along. "Father warned us not to talk about the things that might happen to you in a mill or if you log, Jack. He was afraid that Aunt Ellen would worry too much. You will be careful, won't you?"

"Yes. I'm glad you are worrying about me. But anything can be dangerous, you know. I hope you don't get any more cougars to play with!"

The next day Father said he'd take Jack in the wagon to meet the stage and that his father and mother and Abby could go too. Jack put everything in his blanket and rolled it up. Aunt Ellen wanted him to take a small satchel that she had brought from Vermont.

"For your comb, and that soap Abby gave you, and——"

Jack refused. "I'm going to a mill, or maybe a logging camp, not on a pleasure trip, Mother."

The stage came dashing down the road and into the Mills' yard. While they were waiting for the driver to change horses, Nettie Browning came over to talk.

"Too bad you are going away before the big party, Jack. You know we celebrate the Battle of New Orleans with a dance that lasts almost all night."

"I don't dance," Jack said.

For once, Abby thought that Jack's short answers were perfect.

197

The weather was not only gloomy, but cold. The clouds were black; snow clouds, Father called them. Abby thought it was queer that white snow should make black clouds, but she hoped she might learn why when she went to school. To her the clouds were frowning. Just the right weather for someone to be leaving; Abby liked the weather to match her feelings.

Twelve

They watched the stage jolt out of sight before they went home. The blazing fire and Mother's dinner a little later were very welcome. They had mulligan, one of Jack's favorite dishes, and Abby wished that he could have some.

Aunt Ellen shivered and said she thought the weather was getting worse.

"Almost the end of December," Uncle John reminded her. "When the days begin to lengthen, then the cold begins to strengthen."

While they ate, Abby began to plan for the party in January. "I'll want to wear my new silk, and the locket. Now that I'm fourteen, I'm old enough to dance, don't you think, Mother? Uncle John can take his fiddle and play and teach me some steps in the evening."

"Swing 'em on the corner, like swingin' on the gate. And now your own, if you're not too late." Uncle John shouted like he was calling for a real dance. Abby took Clara to the middle of the room and made her practice the steps.

Father looked out the door. "Henry, I think we'd better batten down the hatches, as our old friend the captain would say. If my weather eye is right, we'll want to have

199

supplies for the stock and for us where we can reach them."

Henry went to the door and sniffed. "You're right, I can smell a storm coming. We'll get everything in good shape."

Abby bundled up and went out to help. She could do some of the regular chores and give them time to haul some hay from the pasture and bring up some shocks of corn. If these were stacked in the barnyard they would be easy to feed.

She gave the chickens some warm water and some extra feed. Tilly was quacking mournfully so she stopped to pet him and put more corn in his pen. She was glad that the pets were gone, even if the pen did look lonesome without them. They had had time to get used to the woods before the cold weather.

By the time they were eating breakfast the next morning, Father's prediction had come true. Snow was coming down steadily.

"There's time to get another load of hay," Father said. "I'd rather have too much than not enough."

By noon Abby was out shoveling a path to the woodshed. She liked working in the snow, but Father made her come in before dark; he said that he and Henry could do the chores. She brought a pan of clean snow into the kitchen and Aunt Ellen dribbled thick sirup over it. Abby and Clara stuffed so much of it they could hardly eat supper.

Uncle John told her to work on algebra; that was hard

enough to do that she wouldn't fret about the weather.

When they looked out on Sunday, there was only whiteness on the ground. The trees were beautiful, with great loads of snow bending their branches. Father watched to see that the snow wasn't freezing to the limbs of his fruit trees, so that they might break. He and Henry spent a good deal of time keeping a path clear to the barn and woodshed. Uncle John insisted that he could do the milking.

He carried the pails of foamy milk to the North Room and Abby followed him in to help strain it.

"Look around," she said. "Do you remember what I told you? The North Room will take care of us; we won't have to worry about food."

Monday was gray, and snow still fell.

"Good thing Jack went on Friday," Uncle John said. "He couldn't get through if this keeps up."

"I hope he's all right," Aunt Ellen sighed. "Abby, this would be a good day for you to learn a poem for your literature lesson. Let's take this one from Whittier. He wrote it about New England, but it's good for Washington Territory, it seems. Did you know that your grandmother Conner met Whittier? He came to the little village in Vermont where she was teaching."

" 'The sun, that brief December day . . .' " Abby read the poem through and then learned it while she churned.

Father said he would make a trip to the store for such things as tea and sugar for fear the roads might get worse.

"Then if we have to stay home, we won't care. Julia, you make a list. Do you have plenty of horehound and licorice? If we get colds or coughs, we depend on your cough sirup. I know you have herbs."

He came in smiling in the afternoon. "Here's news! The stage managed to get through with the mail. Magazines, a newspaper—well, here is a letter for you, Ellen!"

"Will, don't tease," Mother said.

Aunt Ellen grabbed it. "From Jack!" She read it through to herself, then twice out loud to the others. At supper she read it to them again, so Abby knew it by heart by that time.

He wrote:

Dear Mother,
We made good time getting here. Have a good place to stay. Mr. Crosby gives me room and board and six dollars a week to start. The food is not as good as you and Abby cook, but I won't starve. Tell Abby not to forget what she promised to do. Your loving son,

Jack

Uncle John chuckled. "He'll never write a book; doesn't know enough words."

"What did you promise him, Abby?" Clara asked.

You never could tell what that child would hear, Abby thought. "Oh, about school—and things. . . ."

By another day it was plain that there would be no big party. "You see what happens when you are persistent," Abby said. "The snow doesn't make any fuss about it, just keeps quietly coming—and look how it piles up!"

Father and Henry celebrated New Year's Day by shoveling paths to the barn and stables and getting food and water to the stock.

"Lucky I put up so much hay last summer," Father kept saying through the next week. "But this isn't as bad as the first year we came. Remember, Julia?"

"I'll never forget," Mother answered. "The weather turned cold in October. By November the Chehalis River was frozen two feet down. Then came the snow, and it stayed on until March."

"Julia! I didn't know you ever had such weather out here."

"I wrote about it, but that was when John was in the hospital and you didn't worry about anything else. There never had been such a winter before, and probably never will be again."

"That's true," Father assured her. "We don't need to worry. For one thing, the ground isn't frozen as it was then under the snow. Now the cattle could paw away the snow and get some grass if they had to. I don't think this will last more than a month."

"Neighbors all helped each other," Mother said. "But they couldn't do enough, and when the snow went away in the spring there were dead cattle and horses over the fields."

Abby didn't see why her father and mother went on and on with these doleful stories. Aunt Ellen was already worried about Jack; no use making her any worse. She would ask her aunt for a lesson; that took her mind off Jack and the snow.

Once when Father had let her go out to feed the chickens and see the ponies she told him and Henry what was worrying her. They agreed to help out and tried to think up funny stories to tell Aunt Ellen. Father asked Uncle John to play dance tunes and he and Abby, and sometimes Mother and Aunt Ellen, would go through the steps. They popped corn and made taffy, so it was almost like a party every night, Abby thought.

She was sure that there never were better teachers than her aunt and uncle. Everything was fun the way they taught it. Aunt Ellen read poems to her, and had Abby learn and recite them. She helped to write little stories. Sometimes in the evening they read *David Copperfield,* and while it was sad, it was about people so far away that Abby would only have a kind of pleasant cry about them. They read the book about Mrs. Bates' adventures on the Pacific coast, but Mother wouldn't let them read it in the evenings; there were too many killings in it. She said they would all have bad dreams. Abby was afraid that Mother thought Henry should not have bought it, but Abby knew that Henry didn't know, since he couldn't read much. Anyway, it was a true story, and Abby thought it was the right thing to study history, even if it wasn't always funny.

She and Uncle John had a history game that always made fun. He would say a sentence and then Abby tried to make one that rhymed. After she practiced a little, she could go fast. One afternoon the two were peeling apples for pies and Uncle John began:

"Let's try the presidents and see what you can do. George Washington was first in line."

"The people thought him very fine."

"His terms in office were but two."

"And all were sad when he was through."

"John Adams next—a stormy term."

"His acts—that's a hard one, Uncle John. I can't think . . . Yes, here you are . . . His acts made the Republicans squirm!"

The days didn't seem long enough to do all the things that they planned. Mother gave Abby quilt blocks to sew in the middle of the day, when the light was best; in the evenings she had her practice knitting, since she soon learned to do that with little light. Abby's ambition was to be able to knit as fast as her mother and aunt did, and to look around while she worked. Now she still had to watch her stitches.

Father read the newspapers that he had over and over, for all through January the roads were blocked and no mail came through. Uncle John said he was sure that was a great relief to Jack, for he didn't have to write any letters. But Abby knew that he was wishing he could hear.

Thirteen

Abby was figuring on the almanac one morning. "Mother!" she called. "Did you know that today is the second of February? January has gone, fast. We've done the same things over and over, but the days went by in a hurry. I've learned more in this snowed-in month than I could in a year at school. Of course, I must go to school to learn other things," she added hastily. Then she sighed. "Uncle John, even if I can pass the examinations, maybe Father won't have money enough to send me away to school. I'm afraid it costs an awful lot."

"I've been thinking about that, Abby, and I have an idea. Please bring me your Queen Susan box."

What that might have to do with money, Abby couldn't see, but she went to the mantel. Before she picked up the box, she looked at the little Chinese figures that she kept near it. "I love my Chinese figures, Henry," she said. "I let Clara look at them when I hold them, but she is not to play with them."

Clara looked up from her corner. "I haven't time to play. I am teaching my baby to read, and to spell." The doll that Aunt Clara had given her for Christmas was seldom far from Clara, day or night.

Abby handed the box to her uncle and he opened it.

"Did you ever show these trinkets to Mr. Lum?" he

asked. "I know that museums buy things like these. There can't be very many of these trinkets the Hudson's Bay Company used for trade, like these beads and gewgaws from Montreal. Look at these beaded headbands and moccasins and this tiny basket. And the earrings and etched copper bracelets can't be just common stuff. I think that you could get money for them from an eastern museum."

She shook her head. "They were presents to me; I couldn't sell presents."

"If a wealthy grandmother left you money, you would use it for school, even if it was a present. Queen Susan loved you, so I think she would want you to use them to make you happy."

Henry examined the trinkets. "These copper things came from near Victoria, I'm pretty sure. I know it was nearly one hundred years ago that the English traders brought sheets of copper and traded for beaver skins. The Indians on Vancouver Island made good jewelry. I think your uncle is right, Abby, these may be worth money, and you ought to sell them."

"Well, when I get a chance I'll take them to Mr. Lum and see what he says." She looked out the window. "This day is over and we haven't had a bit of sun."

"That's good," her uncle said.

"Good? Why?"

"This is the day the ground hog came out. He didn't see his shadow, so he didn't go back into his burrow. Now we'll have spring."

Clara looked out the window. "Where is the ground hog? I want to see him."

Abby laughed. "Goosie! Uncle John is teasing."

"He's right, though," Henry said. "I could feel spring today; this snow won't last long. I must get busy on my nets that Jack started. He promised that he'd take a week off and come home so he and I could go to the Cowlitz for the smelt run."

"Smelt run—what's that?" Aunt Ellen asked. She had looked up as soon as Jack's name was mentioned.

"Smelt are a little fish like sardines," Henry answered. "When they run in the spring you can stand on the riverbank and dip them out by the tubful. I'll get some dip nets ready. Those little fish make mighty good eating."

"That reminds me," Mother said. "We have a few left that we kippered last spring. If you think it won't be long before you get a fresh batch, I'll use these up; we might have them for supper!"

Abby lifted the lid of the Dutch oven. "That Indian pudding is almost done, Aunt Ellen. Shall I get the table set?"

"Listen!" Henry went to the door and opened it. He held his hand high. "Wind coming up; Chinook."

Aunt Ellen was curious. "Chinook? An Indian?"

"Chinook is a wind that takes the snow away," Father explained. "Sometimes it works too fast; that means floods."

"I'm glad that we are on high ground," Mother said. "I can't understand why some people live in the valley and have to get out year after year when the river rises. They keep a rowboat tied to their back porch. If the river comes up and floats it, they get in and row away with whatever they can carry."

Her sister protested. "Julia, now you are starting to tell yarns, and I thought I could trust you."

"That's really true, Aunt Ellen," Abby said. "And I think that Mother is absolutely right. You know I always say that the best place for a house is up by the old fort."

"Chinook or not," Uncle John said, "let's get supper over with. This is the evening Miss Abigail Conner takes an examination in algebra."

While she took her "examination" in algebra, Abby could hear the wind blowing. Once she stepped outdoors, and the wet wind cooled her cheeks. It does smell like spring, she thought. Henry was right, spring is coming soon. Spring would bring the work she liked—planting garden, setting hens—work that meant food for the winter and money for school. Then there would be the flowers; the white trillium through the woods. They came so suddenly that she thought if she sat and watched she might see them grow. The Indian pipe, with its brown and cream markings, was a favorite too. And the tiny yellow violets—she shook herself. As Mother often said, she liked to plan ahead when she ought to be doing the present work. Just now that was algebra; she went back in and tackled a problem that had seemed hard, but now came out fine.

Aunt Ellen was surprised when she looked out in the yard the next morning. "Why, see, the ground around close to the trees is bare already. That chinook, if that's what you called it, certainly worked all night."

The soft chinook wind kept on blowing, and in a day brown patches began to show between the snow-drifts. They grew larger each day; the snow simply vanished.

"Lucky the ground didn't freeze before the snow fell," Father said. "This way, the snow melts and soaks in and doesn't run off to do a lot of damage in flooding. Now it feeds the underground rivers that make our springs and our wells."

The wind must be carrying the snow to another country, Abby thought. It disappeared so completely. Then one evening a gentle rain began, and by the next day the only traces of snow were in the gullies that were protected from the wind.

The first stage that came through brought a letter from Jack.

Dear Mother and All,

I hear that you are snowed in. That is why it is better to live on Puget Sound; water roads can't be blocked with snow or mud. We go out every day in the rowboat, and several Sundays we took trips in Mr. Crosby's sailboat. Once we went to a place called Oakland Bay. It is the county seat of Mason County. I will tell you about that trip when I come home next month.

Your loving son,
Jack

Uncle John laughed. "Must be excited about something; writing a long letter like that!"

"He seems to have changed his mind about boats; he always claimed he didn't like them," Abby said.

Aunt Ellen began to figure. "He says 'next month' and now it's past the middle of February—he could be coming soon. I wonder whether he is quitting there. He doesn't say anything about going back."

Henry shook his head. He was sitting near the fire and working on his nets. "No, he's just going to take a week off. He knows it's almost spring and he's coming up here to go fishing with me. Abby, you write and tell him that the smelt run will be early in March, remind him that he promised to go with me."

Abby didn't think that was why Jack was coming. "He's right on the water; he can go fishing better there. Bet he's getting lots of clams and fish. Oysters, too. I read in the Olympia paper about the oysters at Mud Bay; that's not far."

"No," Henry said, "can't get any smelt at Mud Bay. You write and tell him about the smelt. That's easy fishing."

Father had another idea. "I hope he takes some time off the last of March to help with the garden work."

"One thing about Jack's letters; they are so short that we can do a lot of figuring on what he means. But don't count on his helping with the garden, Will, he never liked that work. And that reminds me," Uncle John went on in the low voice Abby knew meant he was very serious, "did you tell me that your property line runs quite near this house?"

"Yes, when we took the claim, we decided to build on this knoll because there is a little view over the valley. Later, we found out that the Duncan claim joins ours about a hundred feet from the house. Why do you ask? Unless he builds directly by the boundary line, I don't think it will matter."

"Duncan was in the mill today," Uncle John explained. "He is going to the Colville mines and wants to sell his claim. Seems Stearns will buy the low part, where the best crop land is, that joins the old Judson place that Stearns bought. But he doesn't want this hill part next to your place. . . ."

"If you bought that you could build near the line and we would be close together!" Mother was so excited she could hardly talk.

"That's the way I figured it," Uncle John said. "I took an option on the upper eighty. I didn't want to do anything final until I talked to Ellen and Jack. As for me, I'm all for it. That hill would graze a little stock. I can't do much real farming, and I'm sure that Jack doesn't want to. But I could raise a good deal of our food."

"You mean our house would be on our own land, but just a little way from here? Oh, Julia!" Aunt Ellen gave Mother a hug.

"I have an idea." Henry spoke up. "Something that's not here on the Conner place but I think would grow on

212

that hill land is grapes. It lays just right, to the west and south."

"I know that fruit trees would do well there," Father said. "We ought to have some more; we could go partners, John. Like Stearns says, that's not grain land, but fruit would do fine on a slope like that."

Aunt Ellen interrupted. "Let's not plan too much. I want Jack to be satisfied, and I have an idea that he is coming home now to say that he wants to go back to Kansas. This snow and storm have probably made him want to leave. In spite of the rain, I'll admit that I want to stay." She smiled and put her hand on Uncle John's shoulder. "But Jack is young; it's his future that matters."

Abby knew that Aunt Ellen wanted to stay because Uncle John was happy here. But, just as when they came five months before, she always wanted to know what Jack would say. They'd have to wait until he came home to know. Abby wished the time would go faster, still, if it was going to be bad news, she would rather have the days drag. If she didn't know, she could always hope.

Fortunately, there wasn't time to worry too much about the future; there was so much work to do as the days became suddenly long and warm. Work outdoors was calling, and it didn't have to call twice to get Abby to answer. She loved this time of year. The garden, the orchard—everything was getting ready to fill the North Room again.

The peach and the early plums were already in bloom. Abby was glad they were near the house; she could stand at the edge of the forest and look at the dainty pink of the peach against the brown logs. The plum trees looked like snow with the green firs behind them.

When she told Father what a pretty picture it made he chuckled. "I didn't plant them there just to make a picture. I put the peach near the house so it would be protected from the north wind. Peaches are like some people, always in a hurry, no patience. They blossom out and then a late frost comes and pinches them."

"Won't be a late frost this year," Henry insisted. "Early spring; already the bees are humming around."

"Every one of the bushes you brought from Olympia last fall is budding," Mother said. "I was worried when the snow came, but I guess it made a good blanket."

CHAPTER Fourteen

Abby had no more long evenings with schoolwork, but she tried to think of some of the things she had learned and say them over as she worked with her chickens, or started the garden. Uncle John was as proud as she was about her algebra examination grade of 93. He said he had made it hard, and he knew she could pass any test.

Mr. Browning had sent to Portland for seeds. Father said Abby always had good luck with seeds, so she could start them. She put cabbage and parsnip seeds in a box in her bedroom window. Then Henry helped her get a small garden plowed and fertilized, ready for the little plants. She marked off straight rows and planted radish and lettuce and early peas.

After supper one warm evening near the middle of March, she wandered around the yard looking at the growing things and keeping her eye on some broody hens. She had put settings of eggs under them that afternoon and wanted to be sure that they wouldn't leave their nests and go off to roost. She knew if they stayed on until dark they would settle down for three weeks.

She jumped when she heard someone behind her say, "Hello!" There was Jack.

Abby was so glad to see him that she almost hugged

him, but she was sure he wouldn't like that, and she didn't want anything to spoil his visit.

Even if he had come home to say that he was ready to go back to Kansas, she was going to be pleasant. She thought he had changed in two months. He looked happier. Probably he was feeling rich, with the money he had made trapping, and now with what he had earned at the mill. She sighed. Now everything would be settled. As long as things were unsettled, a person could always hope for the best. She stared and stared, trying to find out what he was thinking.

He laughed. "Don't you know me?"

"Jack, I'm glad to see you—but you look old, or something. Have you seen Aunt Ellen? Do you like your job? Did you have fun in Olympia? Have you——"

Jack interrupted. "That's better. Now I know you haven't changed; you can still ask a dozen questions to a minute. No, I haven't seen anyone. I went to the barn the back way, and saw you here in the garden. Let's go in."

Mother was spinning and Aunt Ellen was knitting when they saw Jack and Abby. Aunt Ellen nearly knocked the wheel over getting to her son. There was a hubbub of questions so nobody knew who was asking what.

Jack turned to his father. "I thought you would ask me how I got here in the evening, Father."

"I was waiting for my questions until the women were done," Uncle John answered. "But how did you?"

"On my horse! I paid an Indian boy ten dollars for

216

the prettiest little cayuse you ever saw. Now I have him broken, he can't be beat. Kumtux and I will race you and Kloshe tomorrow, Abby."

Kumtux, Abby thought. That means "to understand." But I don't understand. Is he going to ride back to Kansas? What about Uncle John and Aunt Ellen . . . No, she'd keep her resolve not to ask questions. She would listen to what he told the others. She tried to sound cross. "I suppose you still like to eat?"

"Bring the North Room in!" Jack opened the blanket roll he had brought in and began to take out packages. "Mother, here are some pretty handkerchiefs I saw in Mossman's store. Uncle Will, I knew you would like a newspaper; here is the Seattle *Post.* Father, I remembered that you had to sell your chess set when we left Kansas. I found a piece of seasoned maple and whittled you a set." He gave a large package carefully to Uncle John. "Henry, I brought you a knife—you know you lost your favorite when we were hunting."

If I cared to tease, I'd ask Jack who taught him to talk, Abby thought. But it's better to be sure everything stays pleasant.

Uncle John held a chess piece up for Father to see. "Look, Will, a log cabin instead of a castle. Jack, this is the nicest present . . ." His voice seemed choked.

They all crowded around to see the rest of the set. Instead of a king and queen Jack had carved a woman wearing a sunbonnet and a man in rough trousers and shirt. The bishops were Indians wearing blankets.

217

"I'm sorry I had to make plain pawns, Father," Jack said. "When I have time I'll carve some figures."

"I knew you were pretty good at whittling, Jack," Henry told him, "but this is very good work."

Father turned the pieces over in his hand. "Must have taken all your evenings."

"No, but I've been gone more than two months. Didn't anybody miss me?"

"Here's your supper, Jack," Abby called.

Before he came to the table Jack gave Mother a wool scarf and showed Clara how to spin a top he had whittled for her. I guess he forgot me, Abby thought. But as Jack sat down he laid a small book on the table.

"I knew nothing but books would please you. Poems."

Abby blinked her eyes rapidly. Was there ever a prettier book? The cover was dark green leather. "Tennyson's poems! Your mother has taught me some; I love them." She felt the softness of the little book and whispered, "Jack, you oughtn't—this cost money. . . ."

"Money is what I work for, remember? Comes right handy, too."

Father looked up from the paper. "Listen, here's an advertisement about a bargain. If you pay a year's subscription ahead of time, the *Saturday Evening Post* will give you fifteen months for the year's price of $2.50. And they throw in two books free. One of them is *Under the Ban,* by Amanda Douglas. Might let Julia and Ellen read that when they get their work all done. Abby, I put away the money I didn't spend on a trip to Olympia for you, thought I'd buy you something. What about a magazine subscription?"

"Father! That's just the thing."

"As Abby's teacher I suggest the *Youth's Companion*." Uncle John made it sound important. "They tell about new books, and besides stories they always have some instructive articles."

"Sam Woodruff has a good bookstore in Olympia," Jack said.

Abby thought he seemed very much at home in Olympia but wondered how he happened to know about a bookstore. "When I get to go to Olympia I'll spend some money in his store," Abby said. She was looking at her new book. "Did you get this there?"

"Yes," Jack answered. "But when you go to Olympia you'll see so many interesting things you won't want to waste your money on books." His grin was friendly. "Henry, have you seen Mr. Lum lately? Any money for me? I'm still after *hiaqua*, you see."

"Yes," Henry replied. "I was down there today. He said for you to come to see him when you came home. He has seventeen dollars for you, but he wouldn't send it; wanted you to come after it and visit. Abby, I forgot to tell you at supper, Lum said he had heard from the museum people in Washington and they'll buy some of Queen Susan's trinkets but they'll have to see them to know what they are worth. Lum says he'll pack them for you if you like. He is sure you can trust the Smithsonian to do the right thing."

"Queen Susan?" Jack asked.

"I'll tell you about it someday. It means—well, let's not talk about it now." Abby was sure that if she did mention that this was money that she wanted to help her go to school, Jack would begin to talk about the Watsons' leaving to go back to Kansas.

"Hurry and eat so you can sit here and tell us about your work," Aunt Ellen said.

Father had been reading while the others talked, and now he broke in again. "Listen to this. Probably was a good thing they got the university at Seattle, after all, instead of out here at Boisfort. Nobody ever thought Seattle was much of a place, but it's picking up. They tell about their ships to San Francisco and across the Pacific to China and Japan. Some, I guess, go round to New York. Here's what I was reading, tells about the university. 'Rooms free at the President's. Bring bedding and furniture. Government firm, but parental. Particular attention to morals.' Might be a good place for a fourteen-year-old girl, Julia. What do you think?"

Mother was rocking Clara to sleep, so she only smiled and nodded. A knot came in Abby's throat when Father said, "I'll write and ask them about examinations and terms for tuition."

She wished he wouldn't talk about it. If they planned as if she might go and then she didn't—well, she couldn't stand it. It had been hard enough to give up the Olympia trip after it was planned, but this—going to school—she had never thought she might go to the university. . . .

She pretended to see something from the window, and stood there looking out.

"How's your job, Father?" Jack asked.

Now it's coming, Abby thought. Uncle John will tell him about wanting to buy the upper eighty, and Jack will say no. I won't listen, she decided.

"I have to look at my setting hens," she said, and left.

She stayed outdoors until it was dark, just petting Tilly and patting Prince. They enjoyed this unusual attention. At last she knew she couldn't postpone things any longer and went slowly in. She could hear them talking, but as she came through the door talking stopped. That made her sure they had been talking about her.

Father cleared his throat. "As I was saying, John, everybody will be glad to have the Watsons stay here to live. You sure got a reputation the way you took care of Jack when the bear clawed him. Trouble is, they're likely to call on you every time anyone gets hurt."

Uncle John smiled happily. "You know I'd be glad if the doctoring I learned in the Army could be put to good use."

"Trouble is, no money in it," Father said. "They'd want to give you a pig, or a calf."

"I can use pigs—or any stock."

Queer talk, Abby thought as she cleared the table. But it was queerer when Jack began to talk.

"Mother, you and Father will have to come to visit me at Oakland Bay next summer; I know a little shack I can rent. You'll see why I like living on the water. You

221

know I said I couldn't stand being shut in by trees? Well, there it's like the prairie, you can see for miles across the bay. Wait until you see my view of Mount Rainier!"

Abby put the dishes down on the table and stood and looked at Jack. What had he said? "Visit him next summer." Was he talking about living out here? It couldn't be true.

Uncle John gave the fire a poke and flames made the room brighter. "I'm glad you like living on the water, Jack, and your mother and I will come to see you, but I'm looking forward to my cabin on the hill. Davis tells me that I have credit for a big pile of lumber."

"I plan to stay several weeks, Father," Jack said. "I want to get to camp the first of May. We'll get a yoke of oxen and we can get a place for your cabin, and the orchard cleared. You should see me cut down trees." He swung an imaginary ax.

Henry looked up from the net he was trying. "Don't forget our fishing, young feller."

"Fishing!" Jack boasted. "I can go fishing from the side of the cookhouse any evening! In a couple years I'll buy up some timber and have a camp of my own. You can come up there and fish. But I'm ready to take a few days off for this smelt fishing you talk about."

Abby hadn't moved from the table. When Jack turned and looked at her she said, "Will you please tell me what you are talking about? Where's Oakland Bay? Why are you going there? What——"

Jack interrupted. "Oakland Bay is near Shelton, about

twenty miles by water from Olympia. I'm going there because I have a job in Willey's mill." He put his hand to his head. "Abby, could you look—here, by my forehead. . . ."

She hurried to him. "Jack, does that place where the bear clawed you still hurt?"

"No, but there seems to be something there. Do you feel anything? I wonder whether it could be pitch."

"Pitch?" Abby saw the others were all smiling. "Pitch? What do you mean, Jack? Is it——"

He nodded. "Yes, guess that's pitch in my hair. I suppose I'm stuck out in your Washington Territory for good!"

"Mother"—Abby hated the way her voice shook—"I

guess I'll get us something to eat. There's some pie. . . ."
She hurried to the North Room. Jack followed her.

"Don't forget," he whispered, "you are responsible for
the pitch in my hair."